Dani turned and looked him square in the eye.

"I brought you up to my bedroom, Sullivan. I'm trying on dresses that leave very little to the imagination and I'm doing my best to make you want me the way I want you."

His trademark cocky smile made an appearance— the one that said the universe was particularly good at glossing over his mistakes. He was too handsome. Too likable. The irresistible golden boy, like dessert for breakfast, lunch and dinner. "You want me to show you my intentions?"

Her breath hitched in her throat. "I do."

He placed his hands on her hips, the heat from his palms nearly searing her right through the dress. He curled his fingertips into her flesh and tugged her closer. He trailed one hand to the small of her back and began to drag that zipper down. Electricity danced along her spine as his fingertips grazed her skin along the way.

Their gazes connected. "I want it all," he said. "Everything."

She let the dress drop to the floor, placed her hand on Cole's shoulder and pushed him back onto the bed.

* * *

Secret Twins f
Cattleman's Club: *f*
the century lead

D1042015

Dear Reader,

I'm so excited for you to read *Secret Twins for the Texan*, my first contribution to the legendary Texas Cattleman's Club franchise.

Confession time! This is my first cowboy book. It's also my first secret-baby book (I've written several secret pregnancies). It's also my first book with twins! Let's just say that I don't shy away from new challenges when it comes to writing. That's half of what makes it so much fun.

I dug deep into my childhood for cowboy inspiration, although mine isn't of the Texas variety. Mine comes straight out of rural Minnesota, where my grandparents owned a horse farm. I spent many summer days in the barn with the menagerie of animals that lived there—dogs, cats and, of course, horses. My grandparents had an impressive stable, including a team of Shetland ponies and four Clydesdales.

Of course, my book is not only about horses or cattle or cowboy boots. There's a whole lot of romance and intrigue... Cole and Dani have so much more than secret twins between them. Cole's been hiding quite a powder keg over the six years they've been apart. Only love can tear down the walls he put up, and when they come tumbling, Dani breathes a sigh of relief. Between that and the investigation into the impostor, there's something for everyone!

Writing this book was an adventure and I'm glad you chose to come along for the ride! Send me a note anytime at karen@karenbooth.net to let me know what you think. I love to hear from readers!

Karen

KAREN BOOTH

SECRET TWINS FOR THE TEXAN

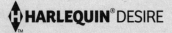

Special thanks and acknowledgment
are given to Karen Booth for her
contribution to the Texas Cattleman's Club:
The Impostor miniseries.

ISBN-13: 978-1-335-97159-3

Secret Twins for the Texan

Copyright © 2018 by Harlequin Books S.A.

Recycling programs
for this product may
not exist in your area.

Printed in U.S.A.

www.Harlequin.com

Karen Booth is a Midwestern girl transplanted to the South, raised on '80s music, Judy Blume and the films of John Hughes. She writes sexy big-city love stories. When she takes a break from the art of romance, she teaches her kids about good music, hones her Southern cooking skills or sweet-talks her husband into whipping up a batch of cocktails. Find out more about Karen at karenbooth.net.

Books by Karen Booth

Harlequin Desire

The Best Man's Baby
The Ten-Day Baby Takeover
Snowed in with a Billionaire

The Locke Legacy

Pregnant by the Billionaire
Little Secrets: Holiday Baby Bombshell
Between Marriage and Merger

Texas Cattleman's Club: The Impostor

Secret Twins for the Texan

Visit her Author Profile page at Harlequin.com, or karenbooth.net, for more titles.

For my Desire author sisters,
Joanne Rock and Cat Schield.
I couldn't have written this book without you!

One

More than anything, Cole Sullivan wanted some dinner. It had been a long day of juggling his two jobs—running the Sullivan Cattle Co., his family's longhorn ranch, and investigating the disappearance of Jason Phillips, which had recently become a murder case. There were not enough hours in the day to be good at one thing, so Cole felt as though he was half-assing everything, and that was not the way he liked to operate.

But before food, he needed a shower. Hours out on a horse had his back in knots, and just as much time on the phone and the computer doing investigative work had his shoulders feeling even worse. He left behind his filthy ranch clothes and walked across the cool Carrara marble floor in his luxurious master bath. This was one of his favorite places to unwind and enjoy the finer things in life. With a turn of the gleaming chrome handle, a dozen shower-heads sprang to life in the generous glass enclosure. He ducked into the hot spray, adjusting a few nozzles to hit his back and shoulders in just the right spots. Drawing in a deep breath, he willed his muscles to do the unthinkable and relax. The stress he was under was not good for him. His doctors would be deeply disappointed to learn how much strain he was put-ting his body through every day. He was practically tempting death. But it didn't matter. Worry about his physical state wasn't going to keep the multimillion dollar family business running, and it wouldn't avenge the death of an innocent man who'd left be-hind a seven-year-old daughter.

"Cole? You in there?" Cole's younger brother, Sam, was yelling out in the hall. This was one of the downsides of having his two brothers living on the family ranch. Separate houses for both Sam and Kane, and even at opposite corners of the sprawling property, but still, very little privacy.

Cole shut off the water and grabbed a thick white towel from the heated chrome bar, another luxury he appreciated greatly on days like today. "Yeah. I'm in here. What's wrong?"

"Nothing. I just meant to talk to you about some-thing today, but we haven't had a spare minute."

And this was my spare minute. "Let me throw some clothes on. Grab a beer or something and I'll join you in a few."

"Got it."

Cole ruffled his hair with the towel, then wrapped it around his waist. Padding into his walk-in closet, he grabbed clean jeans and a plaid shirt, and joined his brother. Sam was out in the kitchen, sitting on one of the eight hand-tooled leather stools at the bar overlooking the center island topped with black Ashford marble. Much like the bathroom, no expense had been spared in the kitchen, with state-of-the-art stainless appliances and—something Cole considered a necessity for his coffee habit—a commercial grade espresso machine.

"What's up?" Cole headed straight for the subzero refrigerator and pulled out the steak he'd been looking forward to all day. He set it on the counter to let it come to room temperature.

"Dani's back in town."

Cole froze for a moment, letting those words sink in. He turned around. "What did you say?"

"Danica? Your ex-girlfriend? She's back in town. I thought you'd want to know." Sam threaded his fingers through his thick brown hair, a shade or two darker than Cole's. His blue eyes were plaintive, as if he expected Cole to accept the truth, regardless of the implications. Five years younger, Sam had a way of just coming out with things. There wasn't much diplomacy.

"Of course I know who you mean." Cole strode over to his brother and folded his arms across his chest. "Back or just visiting?" He hadn't seen Dani in nearly six years. That time had helped dull some of the sting of their breakup, but he lived with the reason for it every day. It was sitting inside his brain, just waiting to kill him.

Sam took a quick swig of his beer. It was the last bottle of Cole's favorite IPA. He never should've been so generous as to offer his brother a drink. "From what I heard, she's back. She's working as head chef at the Glass House over at the Bellamy."

"Not surprising." By all accounts, Dani had been wildly successful in New York. So much so that Cole was shocked she'd ever return. What job could be so enticing as to make her step off a big stage onto the decidedly smaller one in Royal?

"I just thought you would want to know. In case you want to look her up. Or something." Sam shrugged. "I don't know if she's still single, but you are. And I know one thing for sure—you were a hell of a lot more fun when you were with Dani."

"Hey. That's not fair."

"It's the truth."

Cole didn't bother disguising his grumble. "I know better than to go barking up that particular tree. Dani would rather choke me than talk to me."

"Can you blame her? You broke her heart, Cole."

"I had my reasons. You know that better than anyone."

"And six years later, you're still alive while the woman you used to be madly in love with has just moved back to town. Maybe I'm nudging you in the right direction."

Cole shook his head. "I don't need nudging, but thanks. I'll see you tomorrow."

"That's it?" Sam got up from his bar stool and knocked back the rest of his beer, tossing the bottle in the recycling bin.

"The Dani chapter of my life is closed. She moved on and so have I." That wasn't entirely true. He still thought about her, more than he would ever admit out loud. Sometimes he even had dreams about their immediate and sizzling connection. Visions of Dani beckoning him to bed, her silky dark hair cascading over his crisp white sheets, still haunted him. Memories of making love with her were unforgettable—her luscious curves fit too perfectly in his hands to ever erase them from his mind. But she wasn't meant for him, and there was nothing he could do about that.

"You moved on to more work than is reasonable for one person to do."

"I gotta stay busy, Sam. It's the only way I know." Cole didn't need the money he earned from having two careers. Not by a long shot. But he did need to stay occupied. It was the only thing that kept him sane.

"You don't think Dani will come looking for you?"

"Are you kidding me? The woman packed up every one of her worldly belongings and moved halfway across the country three days after I broke it off. That's how far she's willing to go to get away from me." Cole's stomach rumbled. He stalked to the far side of the kitchen and pulled out a cast-iron pan for his steak. "My guess is that Dani will avoid me like the plague while she's here."

"You think you know her that well?"

"I do."

"And you don't want to reach out to her and tell her what happened?"

"No. I don't."

Sam shot Cole that look of pity that he absolutely hated. If he didn't love his brother so much, he might be tempted to knock that look right off his face. "You are a sad case, Cole Sullivan."

"That's life. The sooner you get used to it, the better."

Whether she liked it or not—and she didn't like it at all—Danica Moore could not live in Royal, Texas, and avoid Cole Sullivan forever. She was going to run into him and his handsome face at some point, and it would be ridiculously hard not to slap him. Just imagining the sting of her palm when it struck his chiseled jaw brought a bit of satisfaction, but not enough to undo the pain Cole had caused her. A lifetime of face slaps could not erase that.

Running into Cole's parents or one of his two brothers, Sam and Kane, was just as likely. The superwealthy Sullivans were as ubiquitous in this town as the sun was fierce in July. Dani was eager to avoid any surprise run-ins—too much dredging up of painful memories. His elitist parents' persistent disapproval of her. The accident. Nursing Cole back to health. And a rejection that not only knocked her back on her heels, it left her gasping for what had felt like her last breath.

But she was back in Texas, a state that was in her blood, and there was nothing anyone was entitled to say about that. She wanted her twin sons to know the open sky and fresh air she'd lived off as a child. She wanted them to know the only living family she loved, her aunt Dot and her longtime best friend, Megan Phillips. When Megan told her that the executive chef job at the Glass House at Maverick County's crown jewel, the Bellamy, was available, Dani took her chance to return to Royal. She could keep her career as top-notch chef on track and give her boys a connection to a place she loved deeply. Couldn't do both of those things in New York. Hence, hello, Texas. Again.

But for as many problems as Royal solved, it left her with one—Cole. He was the ultimate loose end. She was already living on borrowed time. She'd been back in Royal for a few weeks. She'd have to see him eventually, so she decided she would see him on her terms. Tonight. His place. He would get no warning. He didn't deserve it.

Dani turned in the mirror, sucking in a breath so deep it was as if she believed the air was made of confidence. Her long black hair was perfect—glossy and full. Touchable. Her makeup was on point, as well. The dress was the cherry on top. Cherry red, to be exact, cut to show off her assets and hugging every curve she'd been blessed with.

She'd worked hard to get back her prepregnancy

body, and she intended to let Cole get an eyeful before she informed him that she'd returned to Royal for good and he was cordially invited to leave her the hell alone. Break a woman's heart and you get the cold shoulder. Or in Cole's case, trample a woman's heart, destroy her illusions about love and leave her knocked up with twins, and you got a four-alarm fire set on showing you what's what.

Dani ducked her head into the bedroom her five-year-old twin boys, Cameron and Colin, shared. She adored this room, with its powder blue walls, the bunk beds the boys had always wanted, and plenty of floor space to play with cars and trains. It was everything they couldn't have in a New York apartment. "Everybody ready for bed?"

Elena, Dani's faithful nanny, looked up from the book she was reading to the boys. "You look amazing," Elena said. "You're going to knock Cole Sullivan dead."

Dani raised a finger to her lips and shook her head so quickly she nearly rattled her own brain. She wasn't ready for Cameron and Colin to know Cole's name. Not yet. They were still so little, so innocent. It wasn't their fault their daddy couldn't be counted on.

"Oh, right. Sorry." Elena's facial expression said more than her words—she understood how important it was to keep the boys a secret from Cole and vice versa. "Boys, hold on one minute. I need to talk to Mommy." Elena got up from the floor and tiptoed over to Dani. "You sure you're not going to tell him?" She didn't need to add the part about the boys. Dani knew exactly what Elena was asking.

"No way. Not today." Dani wouldn't tell Cole anything unless she was completely certain that he wouldn't reject the boys the way he'd rejected her.

"What are you going to say to him when you run into him later and he sees the boys?"

Dani patted Elena on the shoulder. "That's the least of my worries. Cole is so self-absorbed, I doubt he'll bat an eye."

Elena smiled, even though she appeared unconvinced. "I'm sure you know what you're doing." She returned to her spot on the floor to resume story time.

"You boys be good for Elena, okay?" Dani reminded them.

"Where are you going, Mommy?" Cameron asked, ever the chatty and curious one. He looked most like Dani, with dark brown hair and hazel eyes. Colin, her quiet observer, more closely resembled Cole. Lighter hair. Soulful blue eyes.

"I have an old friend I need to go see."

"Why can't we go with you?"

"Because this is going to be boring grown-up talk and I know you'll have much more fun with Elena. Plus, it's nearly your bedtime. Growing boys need their sleep." She knelt down onto the carpet and collected her hugs and kisses. "I love you both very much. See you in the morning."

"Good luck," Elena mouthed.

Dani marched down the hall, snapped up her car keys and slipped through the kitchen to her three-car garage. She'd had nearly six years to stress and worry about the first time she would see Cole again. If she stopped to think about it for too long, she'd put it off, and she didn't want to do that. She knew the exact message she wanted to send tonight, which meant leaving the minivan parked right where it was and choosing to climb into her latest purchase, a treat for herself, a silver Porsche convertible.

Dani had always loved cars. She got it from her dad, who had been a police officer. Ten years gone and Dani still missed him like crazy, but zipping around in this little sports car made her feel closer to his memory. He'd taught her to drive stick. He'd taught her to be a great driver. All those years in New York had meant too many taxis and subway rides. Dani liked to think that her new car was a perfect metaphor for her new life. She was in control now. Completely.

She pulled out of the circular flagstone driveway, the engine purring. The Texas ash and bur oak trees dotting the perimeter of her two-acre property were lit up by the landscape lighting below. The night air was warm, but she could tell that fall was on the way. The days were getting shorter and the mornings a tiny bit cooler. As she drove away from her house, Dani still couldn't believe it was hers—six bedrooms and a nanny suite, tall leaded-glass windows and yellow jessamine vines climbing the trellises next to the arched front door. There was a big pool for the boys out back, and she was having a play structure put in next week. It was perfect, and she'd earned it all on her own.

As she pulled past the guard gate at the entrance to her neighborhood, she couldn't quite believe that, either. Pine Valley was an ultra-upscale gated golf community, the exact opposite of the neighborhood she'd grown up in. Having had a dad in law enforcement and a mother who struggled to keep a job, Dani grew up modestly. They weren't poor, but they weren't well-off by any stretch. Dani still naturally gravitated toward the clearance section in a department store if that was any indication. Even now, when she had money.

The drive out to Cole's ranch gave Dani the perfect opportunity to rehearse her speech, but every time she started it, she tripped over her words. The trouble was imagining what it was going to be like to finally face him. If he cracked his heartbreaker smile, or looked too closely at her with his piercing blue eyes, she could easily be a goner. If he touched her with his strong hands, she'd melt into a puddle. The love and passion she shared with Cole had once run so deep. Ignoring that would not be easy. Which meant she needed to give him the news in as direct a fashion as possible. "Cole, I'm here to tell you I'm back. And I don't care if you don't like it. If you leave me alone, I'll promise to do the same for you." That could work. Now she hoped that she could deliver it as smoothly as that.

Dani flipped on her blinker and turned on to the road out to the Sullivan family ranch. Just being on the outer edges of their massive property, miles and miles of some of the most gorgeous ranch land in this part of Texas, made her nervous. It was a big reminder of the deepest divide between her and Cole before he'd dumped her—his family was royalty here, with enough money to never think about it twice.

She came from next to nothing, and Cole's parents quite frankly had never seen the appeal of Dani. His mother had even once told her that she didn't think she was good enough for her son. Dani had kept that tidbit to herself, deciding at the time that love would conquer all and she would eventually win them over. That day never came. Cole broke up with her a mere six months later, and the memory of that interlude with his mom became fuel for Dani's quick exodus from Royal. She knew when she wasn't wanted and always acted accordingly.

Dani passed the opulent main gates to the Sullivan Cattle Co. property and instead drove around to the smaller access point used by the ranch hands and delivery people. She would've preferred to make a grander entrance, but she remembered the code for the side gate, not for the others. That was how far she'd been pulled into Cole's life, and just how far she'd been flung out. Still, her heart was pounding when she pulled up to the keypad and pressed the square silver buttons. Knowing her luck, Cole had changed the code.

Wouldn't you know, the iron gate creaked and rolled across the driveway. Dani decided to take this as a final sign. Today was the day she was meant to do this. The sun was still setting as she approached the house, leaving behind gorgeous wisps of red and orange set against that vast black Texas sky. Dani had always loved this house, even if it was a bit over-the-top. There were nearly a dozen peaks in the roofline, too many windows to count, and a wide porch suitable for your fifty closest friends to pull up a rocking chair and sit a spell. It wasn't even the best view on the property, either. The vista out behind the house was even better—with a sprawling flagstone patio and pool and the perfect sight lines to enjoy the gorgeous pastoral scene.

Dani pulled up in front of the main house and parked. She checked her hair and lipstick, then flipped up the visor. She'd better get going before she chickened out. She marched straight up the porch steps and on to the front door. As nervous as she'd been to punch in the code at the gate, ringing the doorbell felt one hundred times more harrowing. The chime was so loud, she could hear it clearly right through the door. She turned away and stepped to the edge of the porch, surveying the crushed-stone drive that carved its way through the grass for a mile down to the main road. Up here on this hill, tucked away from the rest of the world, she couldn't deny she was happy to be back in Royal. Even with everything waiting for her on the other side of that front door.

She turned back and took another try at getting someone to answer, this time jabbing the doorbell twice. She stood up on her tiptoes and looked through the glass at the top of the heavy wood door. In that instant, her eyes met Cole's as he strode through the front hall.

Shoot.

She dropped down to her heels. Her heart was hammering like she'd just run to the house instead of driving. She pressed her hand to her heaving chest and backed up to the middle of the porch to give herself some space. *Short and sweet. Keep it simple and get the heck out of Dodge.*

She forced a smile as he opened the door but quickly realized just how pointless her preparations in the car had been. She was in no way ready to be in the company of tempting and towering Cole Sullivan. Not his muscular shoulders or broad chest. Not his haywire brown hair, so thick it had no choice but to stand nearly straight. And good God, it was damp. Had he just taken a shower? She was not ready for those ice-blue eyes or his tanned skin or the way his lips were slack and questioning right now. She was not yet ready to handle the way he was blinking at her, in utter shock. How could anyone make confusion so sexy?

"Well, well. If it isn't Dani Moore. I heard you were back in town." His voice was all swagger and ego, and that just made her mad. Of course he already knew she was back. How could she have been so stupid to have thought any less of him? Cole stepped over the threshold, leaving him a single stride away.

Instinctively, she took another step back. She could feel exactly how drawn she was to him. Her body wanted nothing more than to press against the hard planes of his body and kiss him. Her brain was well aware of how foolish that idea was, and it was prepared to do anything to protect her. "Yes. I'm back."

"Six years and you just show up on my front porch?" He shook his head and laughed mockingly.

Dani failed to see what was so damn funny. "Hell, yes, six years and I just show up on your front porch. I was afraid that if I called, you'd lock up the whole ranch so tight no one would ever get in." She sucked in a deep breath to quiet her thumping heart. She could do this. Even if seeing him had her ready to abandon common sense and fling herself into his arms. No wonder she'd been so hung up on him for years. Seeing Cole Sullivan was like coming home.

"So this is a permanent change?" His thick eyebrows drew together, making it hard to answer in a timely fashion.

"I'm the new executive chef at the Glass House."

"That's a pretty fancy gig." Cole leaned against the door frame, crossing his arms over his broad chest. "Of course it'd have to be to pry you away from the glamour of New York."

She pursed her lips. How dare he take that tone? "It wasn't about the glamour. Going to New York was about putting myself on the map in the culinary world. And it was about getting as far away from you as possible."

He smiled wide, and damn if it didn't make the desire to kiss him that much stronger. "Gotta love that trademark honesty of yours. It's refreshing."

"I'm not here to entertain you. I don't want things to be awkward or uncomfortable if we run into each other, and you know how this town is. We'll definitely cross paths. I just don't want any trouble."

"If you don't want things to be awkward, come and have a drink." He gave a nod inside.

"This isn't social hour, Cole. This was supposed to be a quick visit."

He cocked an arrogant eyebrow at her. "If it's not social, why are you wearing a dress designed for stopping traffic?" He looked her up and down, his determined gaze making it feel as though she was wearing nothing at all. "Not that I'm complaining. I've always loved this particular view, and I have to say, it's improved with time."

Heat bloomed in her chest and ran the length of her body. Damn the more girlish parts of her. Why did they have to be so thrilled by the revelation that he thought she looked good? Oh, right, because that had been part of her plan. She'd wanted to mow him over with her assets. Well, good. She'd accomplished that much. "This old thing? I'm still unpacking, and it was the first thing hanging in my closet."

The skepticism was all over his face. "Uh-huh. Well, it seems a shame to put that old thing to waste. Come in and have a glass of scotch"

"No, thank you."

"I have a bottle of twelve-year Johnnie Walker

Black from the '70s. My dad had it in his cellar. I know you love your scotch."

Shoot. She *did* love scotch, and being around Cole had her needing to soothe her ragged nerves. Plus that bottle of water she drank in the car on the way over? It had been a bad idea. She needed to use the ladies' room, pronto. Even so, it didn't matter. This was Cole Sullivan. He hadn't just trampled her heart, he'd driven over it with his big old pickup. She would never forgive him for that.

Anger rose in her like floodwaters. "I told you, no. Don't think that you can just sweet-talk me and I'll be nice to you." She whipped around so fast her skirt twirled. That hadn't been her aim, but it did make for good drama. "See ya around, Cole." She waved, not looking at him, thundering down the stairs.

"Dani. Come back. Stop being ridiculous."

She stopped dead in her tracks. "Ridiculous? What exactly about this is ridiculous? You treated me like crap, Cole. I nursed you back to health after your accident and how did you reward my undying devotion? You broke up with me." With every word out of her mouth, she was only getting more and more infuriated. She planted a finger dead in the center of his chest. "You are a jerk. And I don't have drinks with jerks. End of story."

She reached for her car door handle, but the next thing she knew, Cole had his hand on her arm. His touch was tentative, but it was enough to make her shudder. Her heart fluttered. White hot desire coursed through her veins. He sent a tidal wave of recognition through her, something for which she'd been wholly unprepared.

Two

Cole acted out of pure instinct, tearing down his driveway after Dani. Damn, the woman could run in heels. Luckily, his long legs carried him fast enough to give him an edge and he caught her, wrapping his hand around her arm before she could open the car.

The instant he touched her, he knew he'd made a colossal mistake. He knew it all the way down to the soles of his feet. There was too much fire between them. Always had been and probably always would be. Sure, that had been years ago, and a lot had changed since then, but he should have known better. Still, he couldn't let her run off like this.

"Dani, don't. Please don't leave. It's okay to still be mad."

She whipped around, sending a trail of her sweet

perfume straight to his nose. How could he have forgotten how beautiful she was? Glossy black hair, fiery brown eyes and red lips that could make a man forget what exactly he'd come for. "I do not need your permission to be mad. I'll be mad for the rest of my life if I feel like it."

One thing was for sure—Cole was sorely out of practice in the art of taming Dani. "I know. I'm sorry. You're right."

She tried to wrestle her arm from his grip, but that bit of friction between them—warm skin against warm skin—sent a flood of memories through his brain. Dani had always done this to him. She'd always brought everything back to life. He'd just forgotten how good it felt to have a taste of it.

"Let me go."

He did as she requested, but she didn't move. She didn't immediately reach for the handle on the car door, and Cole decided to take that as a good sign. She wasn't running again. Not yet, at least. "Please come in and have one drink. I want to hear about New York. I want to know what's going on in your life."

"Maybe I don't feel like telling you."

"Good God, you are stubborn." He shook his head. "Probably why I could never quite get you out of my system."

"Yeah, right."

"I'm dead serious. I wasn't kidding about the scotch, either."

She looked away, and the moonlight caught her

profile—an adorable nose that turned up slightly at the end, dark hair blowing in the breeze across her creamy skin. For what felt like the millionth time, he wished he hadn't had to push her away nearly six years ago, but he'd had no choice. Life and death had been hanging in the balance. Her whole future opened wide, and his narrowed to a narrow and finite point.

"I do need to use the restroom," she muttered, seeming embarrassed.

"Perfect. Come on in."

He tentatively placed his hand at the small of her back to usher her up the driveway, but she was walking a pace faster. "I wasn't kidding. I drank an entire bottle of water on the way over here."

Cole laughed and jogged ahead, taking the porch steps in two long strides and opening the door for her. "You know where it is."

She cocked an eyebrow at him. "I do."

He watched her as she walked down the hall, wondering once again if he was seeing things. Dani was in his house. Wearing a dress that hugged every glorious inch of her, especially his favorite parts—her hips, her butt, her breasts. Basically, everything that was lush and round and good for sinking his fingers into. When Sam had told him a half hour ago that she was back in town, he certainly hadn't thought she'd turn up on his front porch. It was like fate was delivering him a gift he had no idea what to do with.

There was no telling how long Dani or her lovely dress were going to stick around. His gut told him he'd better make this good. He hustled into his grand but comfortable living room, with high wood-beamed ceilings and seating for at least twenty people for the rare times when he decided to entertain. He turned off the flat-screen TV above the stacked stone fireplace and switched on an antique bronze craftsman lamp to cast a warm glow, making the room feel cozier. More intimate. He put on some soft music and lit a candle. Hopefully Dani wouldn't use that open flame to set his house on fire. He was straightening the throw pillows on one of the leather sofas when she appeared.

"Company coming over?"

"What kind of gentleman would I be if I didn't make the place presentable?"

"I don't know. What kind of gentleman would you be?"

The question was so heavy with innuendo it could've broken a bone if dropped on his foot. "On the rocks, right?"

"Good memory." She breezed past him and took a seat.

"I only poured you one of these at least a hundred times."

"Probably more like twice that."

"Sometimes we drank beer. Or wine. There was a lot of wine." The undercurrent was that there had been an awful lot of good times between them. Fun times. Celebratory, joyous times. Birthdays. A few anniversaries, even.

There was a lot of history between them, and he knew he had no business dredging it up. Not tonight.

Possibly not ever. Especially not about the reasons he'd had to break up with her. Still, she'd always been his biggest weakness. A drink for old times' sake wouldn't hurt.

He walked over and handed her the drink. She took it from him, their fingertips brushing just enough to send a jolt of electricity zipping up along his arm. She was as sexy as ever, even when she was mad. Maybe *especially* when she was mad.

"Tell me about New York." He took the seat right next to her on the couch. Some habits were impossible to break. Sitting with her like this made him want to put his arm around her, pull her close and kiss her. He needed to feel her soft lips against his and taste everything he'd missed over their years apart. The realization made it nearly impossible to sit still, let alone seem relaxed.

She sat a little straighter. "It was great. I did well for myself. Well enough to buy a house out in Pine Valley."

"Did you take up golf? That's a neighborhood for hitting the links or raising a family. That doesn't really seem like your speed." Maybe she'd changed more than he'd bargained on.

"It's beautiful out there, and it's a gated community. I like feeling safe. Is there anything wrong with that?"

He shook his head. "Nope. Nothing at all." He took a long sip of his drink. "I guess your success explains the zippy little death trap you pulled up in."

"A woman is entitled to buy a sports car."

"Absolutely. Just be careful. One run-in with a semi and you'll end up in traction. Or worse."

"You're one to be giving lectures on driving. I seem to remember you wrapping your squad car around a tree and nearly killing yourself." A dark shadow fell across her face as she turned to look at him. "That's what started the trouble between us, remember?"

He'd walked right into that one. He needed to avoid subjects that could eventually lead to the stupid things he'd done. "I'm not talking about me. And you don't see me driving around in a roller skate."

"It's a Porsche. And it's fun to drive. You should try it some time." She shot him an all-knowing look that made his pants feel a little too tight. "So, she probably shouldn't have said anything, but Megan told me that you're working on the investigation into her brother's murder."

He nodded. "You know, Megan's been through the wringer. It's hard for me to blame your best friend for wanting to tell you everything. But yes, we are keeping a very tight lid on things until we can catch Rich."

"So you think he's still here in Royal? Hiding out? Lurking in the shadows?"

"I do. There's a lot of money that's gone unaccounted for and we know he's not about to walk away from that. The man has no fear. He's proven that he will do anything."

"I still can't believe he stole Will's identity, embezzled all of that money, and then went and married Megan." She shuddered. "It's so scary. I can't imagine what she's going through. I just wish there was something I could do to make it better."

"That's my job. But don't worry. We will catch him."

"Good." She knocked back the rest of her drink and gently set the glass on the table.

"One more?"

"I shouldn't." She looked right at him, her tempting lips within striking distance. He couldn't think of a time he'd wanted to kiss her more, not even the very first time he'd done it, when he was a young Texas Ranger and she was a brand-new chef. Back when their whole lives were stretching out before them and the future seemed ripe with possibilities. "But it's just too delicious to say no."

"That's my girl." He berated himself as soon as the words came out of his mouth. That's what the old Cole would've said. The Cole who'd broken her heart to save her. He got up from the couch and poured them both another drink before sitting back down. Hopefully she hadn't noticed what he'd said.

"It's been a long time since you called me that."

"I'm sorry. I shouldn't have said it."

She took the glass when he offered it to her. "It's okay. It was actually sort of nice to hear." She laughed quietly. "I don't know exactly how pathetic that sounded, but I'm guessing pretty darn pathetic. That's what happens when you go for years being single. You end up a total sucker for sweet things guys say."

His ears perked up at that. Not only was she still single, she'd been that way for a while. He knew he shouldn't take any encouragement, but now that he had a drink under his belt and she was softening her hard exterior, it was impossible not to want her and feel as though he had a chance. "Apparently the men of New York don't know a good thing when they see it."

Her eyes raked over his face. That hot, seductive look made him want to dig his hands into her hair and taste her lips. He wanted to unzip that dress, touch every inch of her silky skin, and get lost in her for hours. "A few have a clue. They just don't manage to have a clue for very long. That's the problem."

"Anybody serious?"

She arched an elegant brow. "You really want to know?"

"I really want to know." Except he didn't. The thought of her with another guy made him want to put his fist through a wall, even when he'd willingly given her up.

She took another sip of the amber scotch and cradled the glass in her hand. "One guy lasted a year. Another chef. Celebrity chef, actually. I doubt you watch the Food Network, but he has a bunch of shows. Taylor Blake."

Cole didn't watch the Food Network, but he'd have to be living under a rock to not know Mr. Blake. He was a big figure in the world of barbecue championships, handsome as a male model and knew his way around the kitchen. He also happened to look quite a lot like Cole. Apparently Dani had a type. "I know exactly who that is."

"Oh. Well, it was a long time ago now. He came close to popping the question, I think, but it didn't happen. Too many career aspirations between the two of us."

Dani had always had big dreams. She'd come from very little and had always been determined that wouldn't define her. Her lofty goals were part of what had made Cole end things with her, even though they were also much of what had attracted him to her. He couldn't guarantee her he'd be around long enough, and he never wanted to hold her back. "I'd say I'm sorry, but I'm not really."

"I'm not sure what that means."

"It means I'm not sorry you're single." The words escaped his mouth before he realized what he was saying. He needed to ride the brakes right now, not rev the engine, even if Dani did make his heart pound in his chest and everything below his waist flicker back to life. He was in the middle of a case, back to putting himself in danger. She'd hated it when he was a Texas Ranger, running around and catching criminals. Now he was back at it as a private investigator.

But that was part of who he was—he'd always had a strong sense of right and wrong and a fierce desire to set things straight. This thirst for justice was fed when Cole was twelve and his parents had some trouble with several ranch hands that were not only stealing from them, they were committing robberies in Royal. The Texas Rangers had solved the case and recovered his parents' losses. In their cowboy hats and holsters, Cole had thought the Rangers were everything he wanted to be—strong, resourceful, and dedicated to seeing that justice was served.

"You're drunk," she said.

"No. I'm not."

She laughed that breathy Dani laugh. "I sometimes think you like to argue as much as I do." She angled herself toward him and flashed her big brown eyes, biting her lower lip. It felt like an invitation, but he wanted a little more. One more sign. "I sort of missed it. I have yet to meet another man who will stand up to me."

"Is that what you want? Is that what you need?" His pulse was thundering in his ears as he waited to hear her response. He was really hoping for *I need you. Right now. Right here.*

"Now where's the fun in telling you what I need, mister? I'd rather keep you guessing. I think I've earned the right to do that."

But he did know what she needed, and what she wanted, at least when it came to the physical. That part had never been a problem between them. In fact, it had always been perfect. Consequences be damned, he decided to dip his toes in this hot water, even if he might end up getting scalded. He lowered his head, eyes open to watch for punches launched, but all Dani did was shake her head.

"You're going to kiss me?"

"Right now." He moved a little closer.

"Right here?"

"Unless you tell me to stop." He was inches away, so close that he felt her warm breath on his lips. Her beautiful skin was calling to him, begging for his touch.

"I suppose one time couldn't hurt."

Dani sealed the deal before he could do it. Cole clamped his eyes shut and wrapped his arms around her, pulling her tight against him. It only took a second until she was bending into him, angling her neck for a deeper kiss. Her lips parted and her tongue sought his. That was all the encouragement he needed. He leaned back on the couch, pulling her with him, until her beautiful body was stretched out over the length of his.

She pulled away for an instant, breathless. "What are we doing?"

"I think you know exactly what we're doing." He hoped like hell she wasn't about to change her mind. He never knew with Dani. He kissed her neck, which was a bit of a low blow. He knew exactly how much she loved it.

Dani groaned her approval. "If this happens, it doesn't mean anything. Not a damn thing, okay?"

Maybe Dani really was a gift delivered by the universe. If he could have her one more time and go back to his miserable life later, it would be the best of both worlds. For both of them.

"I promise. This doesn't mean a thing."

* * *

The heat from Cole's body was making it impossible to think straight, but Dani did manage one salient thought: if she was going to have a meaningless hookup with some guy, Cole was her best choice. There was nothing to lose. Everything had already been lost.

He dug his fingers into her hair, deepening their kiss. Of course she was going to respond in kind. He tasted of her favorite scotch. She'd forgotten how good he was with his tongue. He was bringing to life parts of her that had practically closed up shop. He drew a line down her spine but kept going, tugging up the hem of her dress, dragging his knuckles along the backs of her thighs. The air was cool against her skin when he had the fabric up around her waist, but then his fingers slipped into the back of her panties and the heat spiked again.

He was hard between her legs. Even through his jeans she could feel how badly he wanted her. It felt like some small measure of revenge to grind against him, knowing she was frustrating him. Unfortunately, her own dissatisfaction was gaining speed.

Cole shifted up onto his elbows, and Dani reared back her head.

"Let's sit up," he said, his voice a sexy rumble. "I want to get to the rest of you."

"Of course." She hopped up and Cole straightened to sitting.

He curled his finger. "Come here." His voice was low and rough.

It sent a thrill right through her, but she shook her head. "Not yet."

"Don't tease me, Dani. You'll kill me."

"As appealing as you make that sound, I want what I can get out of this, too." She planted her hands on his thighs, leaning forward and letting him get an eyeful of her cleavage. Then she lowered herself to her knees.

Cole untucked his soft, plaid shirt and tore it open. Thank goodness for pearl buttons. Dani sucked in a gasp when he rolled himself out of the sleeves. How she'd missed his broad chest and the patch of sandy-brown hair. She spread her hands across his firm pecs, loving the way his chest rose beneath her palms. She trailed a finger down his centerline, stopping to trace the contours of his abs. A woman could get lost following those lines. Dani had, many, many times.

When she reached his belt buckle, the metal clattered. She unbuttoned his jeans and drew down the zipper. Cole raised his hips and let her tug his pants down his legs. She placed her elbows on his thighs again, leaning forward and touching him through the fabric of his black boxer briefs. He closed his eyes halfway and dropped his chin to his chest, a deep groan escaping his throat. She loved feeling how hard he was from her touch. She loved knowing that she could still do this to him after all this time.

She pulled the waistband down and took him in her hand, lowering her head and drawing only the tip into her mouth. She stroked and sucked, swirling her tongue round and round. He dug the fingers of both hands into her hair, curling them into her head, raking them through her tresses. She wasn't about to let him reach his peak this way. She just wanted a reminder that she could drive him crazy if she wanted to.

She gently released the suction of her lips. His eyes opened only partway as he looked at her. "You are wearing entirely too many clothes."

She stood and Cole scooted to the front edge of the couch, bracketing her legs with his knees. She looked down at him, watching as he untied the bow at the side of her wrap dress. The reaction he had when the dress fell open was so good she almost wished she had a camera to capture the moment. The lust in his eyes? The craving? It was off the charts. The bra and panties she'd opted for, made of the finest French lace, were clearly adding to the appeal. Dani loosened the other tie and let the dress fall to the floor.

Cole rose from the couch and stepped out of his boxers. He was towering over her, even when she was still wearing heels. All that hard manly muscle pressed against her was enough to send her over the edge. She'd forgotten just how easy it was to want Cole Sullivan.

He wasted no time reaching around and unhooking her bra and dragging it down her shoulders. He gripped her rib cage with both of his hands and rubbed her nipples with his thumbs, sending a ribbon of pleasure shooting down her torso and into her thighs. He lowered his head and drew one firm bud into his mouth, swirling his tongue in circles. She watched him as he nearly sent her over the edge with the simplest touch.

She placed her hands on his waist and felt the raised skin of the scar along his right flank. He jumped a bit and so did she. They looked at each other and she saw it in his eyes—an unspoken acknowledgment of their traumatic past. The accident. The breakup. Everything that ushered in the last five years, one of the most difficult periods of her life, despite the beauty of becoming a mother. This was a mistake. She could not let Cole in. Not like this.

She pushed away from his chest and scrambled around, plucking her clothes from the floor as humiliation washed over her.

"What are you doing? Do you have some place you need to be?" he asked gruffly.

"This is a mistake, Cole. A huge, massive mistake."

"You need to work on your pillow talk." He was just standing in front of the couch—completely naked, no less.

She was not going to let visions of his physique get in the way of her quick escape. She grabbed her fancy undergarments from the floor. What had she been thinking putting these on when she got dressed? She knew where she was going. Cole didn't deserve French lace. He didn't deserve to see her in a potato sack, as far as she was concerned. She gave him everything once—her heart, body, and devotion. He threw it all away.

A bundle of clothes in her arms, she tore off down the hall to the powder room she'd used when she first arrived. She couldn't even look at her own reflection in the mirror. She was too embarrassed and furious with herself. She'd probably spit right into the glass. She sat down on the toilet to pee and stepped into her panties. So much for telling Cole to stay away—she'd swung in the opposite direction, let him take off her clothes and climbed right onto his lap. How dumb could she possibly be?

A knock came at the door. "Dani. Come on. Stop being so dramatic."

Speaking of dumb, what was Cole thinking, accusing her of being dramatic? "Go away. Go upstairs to your room or something. I don't want to see you again." She flushed the toilet to drown out anything he might say in response. Unfortunately it didn't work.

"I want to make love to you, Dani." His voice was louder now, like his forehead was pressed against the door.

"No. You want sex. It was supposed to be a meaningless hookup. Remember? You promised me this would mean nothing." Now that her bra was hooked, she made quick work of wrapping herself up in that stupid, stupid dress. She was going to have to throw it away or drop it at the dry cleaner's and never pick it up.

"Come on. Are you just going to leave me like this?"

Dani grumbled and made a cursory glance in the mirror, just to remove the smudges of mascara from beneath her eyes. She didn't want him to see her looking like a raccoon. "I'm coming out."

"Good."

She stormed right past him, down the hall and back into the living room to locate her shoes. "This was wrong…coming here was a huge mistake. I don't ever want to see you again. I don't want to talk to you. Nothing." She worked her feet into her pumps and made the mistake of looking at him. He was standing there in nothing more than his boxers, still sporting the erection that she was not going to make go away.

He flinched at her words, but they were the only thing that made sense to her right now. "That's a tall order. You just moved back to town. We're bound to run into each other."

Of course that had been exactly Dani's thinking when she'd come over here. Now it didn't seem like such a convenient argument. "You do your Cole Sullivan things, running around catching bad guys and raising cattle with your big perfect family, and I'll do my thing. Hopefully we won't see each other at all."

She marched to the front door and breezed right through. She would've closed it right behind her if Cole hadn't stuck his leg in there and muscled it open. Down the driveway she raced, but she could sense Cole behind her. *Get to the car. Just get to the car.*

She opened the door and climbed into the driver's seat, but this was one hell of a time to have long legs and be driving a convertible. She had to contort her body to get into it.

"Dani, stop."

"Cole, have you lost your mind? You're out here in your underwear."

"Do you honestly think I care about that right now? You come to my house all hellfire and brimstone, and I kiss you and you melt right into my arms. What is going on? I thought this could just be two friends having fun. Getting reacquainted. Apparently not."

"You act like you did nothing wrong, Cole. You broke up with me, remember?"

"You don't know everything."

She turned the key and revved her engine. "I know enough. Good night, Cole." The car jerked ahead a few feet when she let go of the clutch, but then it stalled out. "Dammit," she mumbled under her breath. So much for her dramatic exit.

"Guess I'll see you around town."

"I hope not." She turned the key and the engine purred back to life.

"It's a small town, Dani. You can't hide from me forever."

His voice faded into the black night as Dani sped away, cursing herself for coming out here. Kissing Cole Sullivan and letting him take off her clothes had been a mistake. Granted, loving him had been a bigger one. With two little boys at home relying on her to have her act together and give them a stable life, it was a mistake she couldn't afford to repeat.

Three

Cole loved downtown Royal, but especially when there was a party. The Labor Day celebration, with its food vendors, hay rides and carnival games, was a favorite. It heralded the end of the brutal Texas summer and the start of what he hoped would be a beautiful fall. But first, he and the team had to track down Rich. They had to make him pay for his litany of crimes—Jason's murder, stealing Will's identity, and siphoning off millions of dollars from Will's company and the Texas Cattleman's Club. If he was sent away for all of that, everything would be right with Cole's world. Well, almost everything. Dani coming back into town had turned a few things upside down, namely his ability to think about anything else.

He strolled through the main block, which had been closed off to traffic. He was willing to admit to himself that he was hoping to run into Dani; he just wasn't prepared to say it out loud. She'd consumed his thoughts since the other night, and not just because clothes had come off and she'd left him as sexually frustrated as he'd ever been. Six years had numbed him to the memory of what Dani did to him. She made him feel alive. She might have a terrible attitude 50 percent of the time, but he knew that wasn't what was in her heart. Her exterior was nut-hard, but on the inside, Dani Moore was as soft and tender as could be.

He'd seen that caring side after his accident six years ago, when he was still a Texas Ranger. He'd narrowly survived colliding with a guardrail during a high-speed pursuit. Cole had been carried off in a stretcher with broken bones, lacerations and contusions. After his more urgent injuries had been tended to and he was finally stable, the doctors ordered an MRI. That was when they'd discovered the tumor, an inoperable glioma, square in the middle of his brain.

Luckily, Cole had sent Dani home to get some sleep, so only his brother Sam had been there when he got the news. She wasn't there to hear the words no one ever wanted to hear, especially not from an oncologist. They couldn't remove it. Radiation was unlikely to make a difference. It was likely going to be the thing that killed him, but there was no way to know how long he had. Could be days, weeks, months, years or decades. Plenty of people walked around not even knowing they had one, the doctor had said, which had been of zero comfort to Cole.

Cole swore Sam to secrecy, although Sam had begged him to talk to Dani about it. He knew that Cole had been getting ready to ask Dani to marry him. He'd bought a ring. He'd been about to ask her to build a future with him.

Cole wouldn't hear any of it. That doctor had signed his death warrant. He'd already seen what worry did to Dani. Hell, every time he went out on a call or worked on an investigation, she was a ball of stress. She always hugged him and kissed him fiercely when he made it home safe. Cole understood why. Dani's dad had been in law enforcement and he'd died in the line of duty. She'd had to watch the way her mother fell apart afterward, drinking and aiming all kinds of verbal abuse at Dani. Emancipated at seventeen, Dani eventually ended up with her aunt Dot in Royal. Dani's toughness came from loss. Cole would not let that happen again.

So he'd done the only thing he could think to do. As soon as he was back at home, he'd broken it off. Oh, the anger and fury unleashed that day was brutal. But Cole had taken it. Yes, she'd spent countless hours with him in the hospital, and yes, they'd been together for three years. He'd had to lie and tell her that none of that mattered anymore. He didn't love her. Those were the words that had been the hardest to say.

Of course, Dani had refused to believe him. She'd flat out called him a liar. She'd thrown things at the wall—pillows and books and magazines. So he'd had to double down on his fabrication and tell her there was another woman. That was the beginning of the end. She'd become impossibly quiet. Tears rolled down her cheeks, and she'd called him a cheating bastard. He hated to hurt her that way, but it was the only way to cut things off for good.

Three days later, Dani left for New York. By all accounts from the other night, she'd done well for herself. His plan had worked perfectly. Except he was still waiting for the day this stupid tumor might take his life. And he'd never bargained on Dani ever returning to Royal.

The late-morning sun beat down on Cole's back as he continued his survey of town for Dani. When he rounded the corner near Miss Mac's Pie Shack, he nearly ran square into Vaughn McCoy and Abigail Stewart. They both were grinning ear to ear, Vaughn's service dog, Ruby, between them.

"How are you two doing today?" Cole asked.

Abigail smiled even wider, a feat Cole did not think was possible. She pulled Vaughn closer and gazed up into his face. "We're perfect. Absolutely perfect."

Vaughn took Abigail's left hand and presented it to Cole. "Newlyweds, to be exact." The ring sparkled in the sun as she wagged her fingers.

"Oh, wow. Congratulations! When did this happen?"

"Just now," Abigail said. "We got Judge Miller to perform the ceremony in our backyard." She smoothed her hand over her protruding belly. "We wanted to get it done before this little one decides to make his or her presence known."

Cole wasn't the envious type, but he could feel the jealousy rising up inside him. Vaughn and Abigail had the life he'd always wanted, the one he'd once thought was a done deal for Dani and him. Why did some people get their happy ending while others didn't? He didn't know the answer.

He shook Vaughn's hand. "Well done. I'm very happy for you both."

"When are you going to get around to settling down? Or are the Sullivan boys all committed to being bachelors for life?" Abigail asked.

It would've taken Cole an hour to give the real answer. Instead, he laughed. "If you ask my mother, we're all running on borrowed time. She wants grandchildren yesterday."

"Good to see you, Cole. I'd better get my bride down to the diner. She's already reminded me a dozen times how hungry she is," Vaughn said.

Abigail shrugged adorably. "I'm dying for pancakes and bacon."

Cole clapped Vaughn on the shoulder. "You heard her. Get to it."

Just as the happy couple walked away, Cole spotted Dani across the street. Unless his eyes were playing tricks on him, she was with two small boys. The street was packed now, and he had to wind his way through the crowd, past folks saying hello or wanting to talk to him.

I'm so sorry. I'm supposed to be meeting someone. Yeah, hi. I'll see you later?

Dani and the two boys were turning and walking away from him. He had to hurry. Or maybe just lunge for Dani. Without thinking, he reached past several people and grabbed her arm. The crowd parted and she whirled around.

"Cole? What in the world?" She tore off her sunglasses and nearly pierced his very being with her blazing brown eyes.

His heart was about to pound its way out of his chest. "I'm sorry. I just…" *You just what? Saw her and thought you'd wrap your hand around her?* "I wanted to say hello."

"Oh, well, hi." Dani looked down at the two boys who were right at her hips. One was clutching the skirt of her light blue sundress, the other holding on to her hand.

"Can we talk? Over here?" With a nod, he suggested a bench in front of the Royal Diner.

She pursed her lips tightly. "We said all we needed to say the other night."

He should've known he'd have to put some elbow grease into this. "It's a hot day. Probably not a bad idea to sit and take a break."

"I'm fine. Really."

He pointed down at one of the two boys. "I think he could use some time out of the sun. His cheeks are pretty pink."

Horror crossed Dani's face and she leaned down to check on the boy. "Are you okay, honey?"

He nodded. "Just hot. And thirsty."

"Fine, Cole. But just for a minute." She took the boys' hands and led them over to the bench. They both climbed up and sat, swinging their legs. Dani pulled a bottle of water from her bag and offered it to them.

"Who's this you have with you?" Cole asked.

She hesitated for a moment. "These are my sons. Cameron and Colin."

Her what? Cole nearly had to pick his jaw up off the sidewalk He was as confused as could be right now. Dani had painted herself as a single woman without a care in the world aside from her career. One would have thought the topic of having two children might have come up while they'd talked the other night. Was this why she'd glossed over part of her time in New York? And if so, what was she hiding? He crouched down in front of the boys, knowing he had to play it cool. Dani had little patience for him right now. "Hi, guys. I'm Cole. Now which one of you is Cameron and which one is Colin?"

The boy in the red-and-white-striped shirt thrust his hand up into the air. "I'm Cameron."

"So you must be Colin."

In a blue-and-white-striped shirt, Colin seemed more reticent than his brother. He nodded. "Yes, sir."

Cole peered up at Dani, who was beaming at the boys. "I guess there were a few things we didn't have a chance to talk about the other night."

She cleared her throat. "A few things."

Cole straightened to his full height. Dani was

flat-out stunning today, but he couldn't allow himself to be distracted by the way she looked in that sundress with the skinny straps, all glowing skin and luscious lips. "How old are the boys?"

She took a step away from her sons. "Uh. Four. About to turn five."

Cole turned and looked at them again, doing the math in his head. Like most brothers, they were horsing around, poking and prodding each other. Cole was no expert, but they looked ready to go to school. He wasn't buying the idea that they were four, but he couldn't ask them in front of their mom. "You putting them in kindergarten this year?"

"No. One more year of preschool. They're not quite ready yet."

"I see." He took another glance at them. Their coloring was just like his own. Hair color? Remarkably similar. It was even thick like his, not fine like most young children's. "Your relationship with Taylor Blake must've been a lot more serious than you let on."

"I don't really want to talk about it, Cole."

If he wasn't standing in the middle of a packed sidewalk, Cole would ask Dani all sorts of questions. He might even ask for a paternity test. But he had to be glad that she wasn't kicking him in the shins right now or calling him names. After the other night, he did not think a calm conversation with Dani would be possible, but here they were. He was prepared to do anything to preserve the peace.

But were these boys his? Was it possible that Dani had been pregnant when she packed up and left for

New York? They'd had no contact whatsoever, except for a letter Dani sent six months after she left, asking if he wanted to talk. Unable to open that door and wanting to protect her, he hadn't responded.

He looked at the boys again. There was a feeling deep in his gut that was saying they could be his. Even if that might not be the case, he had to have the chance to get to know them better. They were one half a woman he still cared for very much.

He crouched down one more time. "Do you boys like horses?"

Colin, the quieter of the two, jumped right off the bench, nearly knocking Cole back onto his butt. "I do."

Cameron nodded eagerly. "I do, too. Do you have horses?"

"I do. I have longhorns, too. I even have chickens and goats."

"Do you have a real farm, Mr. Cole?" Cameron asked. It was incredibly adorable how polite these two boys were. Dani had done a good job.

"It's a ranch. A big one. Would you like to come see it some time? Maybe tomorrow?"

Dani stepped forward and placed her hand on Cole's shoulder, digging her fingertips into his skin. If she thought it would dissuade him, she was sorely mistaken. Her touch made his pulse quicken and filled his head with ideas of taking off the dress she was wearing today. "Surely you're busy, Mr. Cole."

He shook his head. "Nope. Not at all. I always have time for some aspiring young ranchers."

"Can we, Mommy? Can we?" Colin was jumping up and down, tugging on Dani's hand.

Cameron got off the bench and joined in. "We never got to see horses in New York."

"We did when we went to Central Park," Dani countered. She was so good at digging in her heels.

"That's not the same. We couldn't ride those horses." Cameron turned to Cole. "Can we ride your horses?"

"A few of them you can." Cole had to disguise his smile. The boys were doing his arguing for him.

Dani dropped her shoulders and sighed. "It'll have to be Thursday. I need to be at the restaurant tomorrow, and I have plans with Megan on Wednesday."

Cameron and Colin began jumping up and down again, squealing with delight.

"What time do you want us?" Dani asked.

I want you any time I can get you. Again, Cole's mind flashed to the other night and how amazing it felt to touch her velvety bare skin. "Nine? Before it gets too hot? We can have lunch. Hungry cowboys need their food."

She rolled her eyes and shook her head.

"What?" Cole asked.

"I'm just trying to figure out how you're so good at talking me into things I don't want to do."

"You don't want your boys to have a fun morning enjoying some of the finest things Royal, Texas, has to offer?"

The smile that spread across her face held a familiar edge. It was as if she was whispering, *Damn you, Cole Sullivan.* Good God, how he'd missed that sight. "No. You're right. It'll be fun."

He reached out and grasped her elbow, trailing his fingers down the underside of her arm. "I promise I'll make it worth your while."

She cocked both eyebrows. "I have two young boys to keep an eye on, Mr. Cole. May I present a prime example of how much supervision they need?" Dani pointed down the sidewalk. The boys had found an older man with a dog several storefronts away. They were gleefully petting it, oblivious to how far they'd wandered.

"I was talking about ice cream. I was thinking we could go out for some after lunch."

Dani pressed a finger, hard, right in the center of his chest. "Don't push your luck."

Cole put his sunglasses back on, feeling as happy as he'd felt in a long time. "I won't need luck. The minute I mention ice cream to those two boys, it'll be all over."

Dani just shook her head and hitched her purse onto her shoulder. "Boys, we should go now," she called.

"Oh, and bring your swimsuits Thursday. I have a slide at my pool."

Dani cast him an incredibly hot look of disapproval. "You're terrible."

"I try."

Four

The day after Labor Day, Cole pulled up outside the Texas Cattleman's Club. This visit was no social call, nor was he here to talk ranching or catch up on the latest gossip in Royal. Cole was here to propose a plan to his team, involving going undercover and hopefully catching Billy Orson, the crooked sheriff who had helped Richard Lowell by falsifying death records and saying that Rich had died in the plane crash that claimed Jason Phillips's life. Orson had received several large influxes of cash since then, which they were certain had come from Rich. It was a bit crazy, but Cole was prepared to do anything to catch Sheriff Orson.

After speaking with Aaron Phillips the other day and then receiving the results of the DNA testing of the ashes in the urn that were once believed to belong to Will Sanders, they knew for certain that it was Aaron and Megan's brother, Jason, who had died in that plane crash. This was a murder investigation. There was a lot on the line, and time was not on their side. Rich was on the run, and it was only a matter of time before he fled the country with the money he'd siphoned off from Will's personal and business accounts, as well as the TCC. They had to catch him. And fast.

But as he strode into the TCC, Cole's run-in with Dani and the revelation that she had twin sons wouldn't stop running laps in his mind. Had his eyes played tricks on him? His gut was telling him no. His gut was telling him that those boys might look like Taylor Blake, but they looked even more like him. And the timeline—especially if Dani was lying— worked. Had she gone to New York and discovered she was pregnant? Was that what the letter she'd sent six months after she'd left was really about? Had it been a call for help?

If any of this was true, he and Dani had a holy mess between them, one that would demand untangling. But for the next hour or so, Cole needed to focus on work. He had to set aside one potential headache for an entirely different one.

He entered a small meeting room down one of the long halls at the back of the building. They were keeping a tight lid on the investigation, but this was the best central meeting place. Too many flapping mouths at the sheriff's office.

Will Sanders was speaking to Sheriff Battle and his deputy, Jeff Baker. Several other deputies were on hand as well, in addition to new full-time members of the task force, courtesy of the FBI—Special Agents Thomas Bird and Marjorie Stanton. Cole had pulled some strings to bring these two on board, but the new DNA evidence had helped convinced the bureau that he needed the extra hands. Bird and Stanton were a crucial part of cracking this case.

Thomas Bird, a reedy man with a thick mustache, was an expert in money laundering, having made his name working on cases involving organized crime. He fully understood the intricacies of the money trail Rich had left behind, especially everything uncovered by Luke Weston's financial tracking software. Marjorie Stanton, a poker-faced redhead, was a tactical expert specializing in sting operations and undercover work. She was also expecting her first child in three months. Her pregnancy had left her doing investigative work and less of the hands-on work she loved. She wasn't happy about it, or so she had mentioned to Cole several times when they'd talked.

Sheriff Battle gave Cole the high sign and informally called the meeting to order. "Now that we have Cole Sullivan on hand, we can get down to business. Cole, why don't you brief everyone on where we stand?"

Cole stood at the front of the room while everyone took a seat. "Sure thing. I believe Deputy Baker has given out the latest brief, but DNA tests have confirmed that Jason Phillips was killed in the plane crash in Durango City, California. We believe Richard Lowell was on that plane and managed to escape. We also believe that he bribed Sheriff Billy Orson to have Phillips's body cremated before it could be identified. Orson identified the body as Will Sanders. Of course, we all know that Will Sanders is alive and well. Shortly before the plane crash, we got an eyewitness report from Abigail Stewart of an argument between Jason Phillips and Richard Lowell posing as Will Sanders. That was the last time Jason Phillips was seen alive. We believe now that Jason was confronting Rich, and that's what got him killed. Although we don't have direct evidence linking Sheriff Orson to the cover-up, it seems pretty clear that he did it. The information given to us by his deputy was invaluable and all pointed to him."

Stanton raised her hand. "This deputy. Is she a credible source? How do we know she isn't trying to lead us on a wild goose chase?"

"Her father was the sheriff before Orson. He was a good man, and she hates seeing her father's legacy ruined like this. She actually put herself in great danger by going to Aaron in the first place. Orson has eyes and ears all over that county."

Stanton nodded and scribbled down a few notes while her partner, Bird, raised his hand. "We're still tracing the payoffs from Lowell to Orson. There's a chance that some of it was cash, but I have to think for this big of a cover-up, it would've been too much money to go that route."

"Orson is a greedy man," Cole said. "He has a massive house up in the hills. He's got his fingers in everything within his jurisdiction. The more I dig, the more dirt I find. All kinds of shady dealings and a lot of evidence of bribes and kickbacks. I'm sure Rich had to make a substantial payoff."

"Everything hinges on Orson right now," Sheriff Battle said. "If we can find a way to get him to talk and admit that Rich bribed him to have Jason's body cremated and falsely identify the body as Will, we could blow the case wide-open."

"And find the money," Bird added. "We still have to find where Lowell has stashed the small fortune he stole. That's crucial to our case against him. A big part of his apparent motive for impersonating Will Sanders was to siphon cash from his personal and business accounts. My search for offshore and shell accounts has turned up nothing. I think we're looking for a physical stash, and my gut is telling me we're looking for gold."

"Really?" Deputy Baker asked. "Isn't that a little impractical? How do you skip the country with gold?"

"It's not about the how. It's about the why. It's the one currency that works anywhere. The disclosure laws are easy to work around, especially if you know what you're doing, and gold is untraceable by electronic means."

This really got Cole's mind going. Did Rich have a stash somewhere in or around Royal? That might explain why they were still sporadic Rich sightings, most recently when Aaron thought he saw Will at the Glass House, when the real Will was miles away at the Ace in the Hole. Was Rich still trying to hide in plain sight, waiting for the perfect time to get to his money? If so, they had to act quickly.

Cole cleared his throat. Time to make his pitch. "Orson is hosting a cocktail party in a few days for potential investors in a pipeline project he's trying to get in his county. It just reeks of more kickbacks and skimming. What if I posed as a bigwig money guy and wore a wire and tried to get him to say something stupid?"

"Yes. That's an amazing idea. I could go with you," Bird offered.

Stanton cast him a doubtful glance. "At a cocktail party for rich people? You're too socially awkward. You'll stick out like a sore thumb."

Bird pressed his lips into a thin line. "Thanks for that."

"Hey. I call 'em like I see 'em." Stanton tapped her pen against her pad of paper. "You need bait. You need a lure. You're a handsome guy, but something tells me you aren't Sheriff Orson's idea of a good time."

Cole leaned back against the wall and crossed his legs at the ankle. "What'd you have in mind?"

"If you do an internet image search for the guy, you get a lot of pictures of him with women, and they are never the same. We're talking a real revolving cast of characters. I think we need to send you with a female. A damn good-looking one." Stanton rubbed her round belly. "I'd do it myself if I wasn't carrying around a baby disguised as a bowling ball."

For a split second, Cole had an idea, but it was crazy. Maybe it was the mention of a "damn good-looking" woman that had him thinking of Dani. But she was a mom with two small kids. That was too crazy to make any sense. He couldn't put her in that kind of danger.

"Sheriff, you have any female deputies right now?"

Sheriff Battle shook his head. "Unfortunately, no. We had one last year but she moved away."

Stanton eyed Cole, but he could see that the gears in her head were churning. "I doubt the bureau will let me steal an extra agent right now. But I can look into it. Otherwise, you might have to find someone, Sullivan."

"You really think it's necessary?" Cole was truly drawing a blank on who he should ask. His brain just wanted to circle back to Dani.

"Honestly? I think it's essential. I don't see you catching this guy without a beautiful woman on your arm."

Dani had really been looking forward to going out to lunch with Megan. Between getting settled in the new house and navigating the landscape of her new job at the Glass House, Dani hadn't had nearly enough time for her best friend. They were supposed to meet up at the Labor Day celebration, but Megan had decided she couldn't deal with questions from well-meaning folks about her husband, the man she'd *thought* was Will Sanders but turned out to be Richard Lowell. Dani still couldn't comprehend the betrayal Megan must be feeling, having built a life with a man who had been lying to her all along. As bad as that was, the death of her brother Jason was worse. Megan knew that he was dead, but most residents of Royal had no idea. Because of the investigation, it had to stay a secret.

Dani pulled into the circular drive in front of Megan's gorgeous French chateau–style home on the edge of town. There had been a time when Dani might've been a little envious of her friend, living in a big beautiful house like this, from the lush landscaping softening the hard edges of the stone facade, all the way up to its grand arched windows peeking out from beneath the roofline. But Dani had made her own strides since she'd first moved to Royal as a teen, and Megan, the beautiful spark plug with deep roots in town, had inexplicably befriended the girl who'd had almost nothing.

Megan came outside, wearing curve-hugging jeans, cowboy boots and a cute black-and-white gingham blouse, along with oversize sunglasses. She had her black designer handbag in the crook of her arm and carried a small soft-sided case in the other hand. "Nice," Megan called out as she approached the car. "You not only brought the convertible, the top's down."

"The minivan makes it hard to pick up guys."

Megan laughed. "Maybe we just keep it to the two

of us today. Men are not my favorite people in the world right now." She leaned over and gave Dani a big hug. "I'm so damn happy to see you."

"Me, too. This was half of the reason to move to Royal—to be able to hang out."

"Not that I didn't enjoy coming to visit you in New York every now and then. That was fun, too."

"What's in the bag?" Dani asked as she pulled out of the driveway.

"You up for a little shooting before we go to lunch? I bought a .380 and I could use some practice. I just joined the Royal Gun Club."

Dani hadn't been to a firing range since her dad had taken her when she was a teenager. "Yeah, sure. Just tell me which way to go."

Dani followed Megan's direction, taking back roads. "The boys and I missed seeing you on Labor Day." Dani raised her voice a bit since the top was down.

"I missed seeing you, too. I ended up holing up in my office and working on new shoe designs. Did I miss any excitement?"

"I ran into Cole. With the boys."

"It was going to happen. I told you."

"I know you did. I just didn't think it was going to happen so soon."

"What happened?"

What *had* happened? Everything had whizzed by so fast, Dani was hardly able to keep up. She'd known that day would come, but just like she hadn't been fully prepared to deal with Cole on her own, she hadn't been ready to see him with the boys. "He's suspicious. I could see it in his eyes." She stopped at a red light. "He asked the boys if they like horses, which of course got them all riled up. I'm supposed to take them out to the ranch tomorrow."

"Great idea. Since your last visit to the ranch went so well." Megan knew that Dani had nearly ended up in Cole's bed the other night and did not hold back on the sarcasm.

"What was I supposed to say to them when Cole offered? I'd already gone and filled their little heads with how much fun we were going to have when we moved to Texas. Getting to ride horses and spend time on a ranch are high on the list of things they want to do." The light turned green, and Dani shifted and sped away. Talking about the visit to see Cole tomorrow had her all tied up in knots. She hated the way she acted around him, almost like she was a different person, casting aside her normally rational thoughts.

"What's your plan then?"

"Honestly, I have no idea. I made a plan for the other night, and it was a disaster. I'm thinking this time, I just go with it."

"Do you plan on telling him someday?"

Deep in her heart, Dani knew she would have to tell Cole, but her protective instinct with her boys was impossible to ignore. Could she trust Cole? She wanted to think she could, but she needed to *know* it. He'd lied when he broke up with her—Megan had snooped and there had been no other woman. Then he'd quit his Texas Ranger job a few months after she went to New York. She'd begged him to do that after the accident, but he'd refused. And of course there was the letter she'd sent about a week before the boys were born, asking him to call her so they could talk about what had happened. She'd meant that as an open door. All he would've needed to do was walk through it. But he hadn't. He'd simply left it to close on its own.

"When I tell him, it'll be for the boys' benefit, not his. I gave Cole plenty of chances, and he hasn't done much good with any of them."

"But he did kiss you. Does that make you think he wants to get back together?"

"No. It makes me think he enjoys kissing me, which does nothing to fix the past."

As Dani pulled into the drive at the Royal Gun Club, she realized she'd managed to avoid the topic of Rich, but she knew she was going to have to bring it up at some point. She couldn't ignore the elephant in the room forever. Megan didn't always like to talk about the things that made her vulnerable, but how could she not be feeling that way? She'd married a man who was assuming someone else's identity, and that man had, in turn, killed her brother. Every nerve in her body had to be raw right now. She was hiding it well, too, which only made Dani worry more.

"I sort of hate to ask this, but did the Rich situation precipitate the gun purchase?" Dani asked as she and Megan walked through the parking lot toward the sprawling one-story cedar-clad building housing the firing range.

"I need to protect myself. It's most likely that he killed my brother. There's no telling what he's going to do next, or who he might go after just to get what he wants."

"That's some scary stuff." Dani could only imagine what Megan was enduring. Dani might've felt betrayed by Cole, but what she'd gone through didn't come close to this. "Are you going to keep the house?" Add that to the list of nightmares Megan was currently living—sleeping in the same house where she and her lying "husband" had once lived as a happy couple.

"Will thinks I should move to the ranch for my personal safety. I don't want to move. I'll feel like I'm letting Rich win if I do that."

Just outside the main entrance to the building, Dani put her arm around Megan and pulled her close. "I'm so sorry."

"It's okay. I'll feel better once I pull the trigger." Megan patted Dani on the back and stepped back. "Plus. I'll be honest. Will's a little too tempting and I'm not ready to go there. The last thing I need is romance."

Dani wasn't surprised. How could Megan not be attracted to the real version of the man she thought was her husband? "You do what's best for you."

Dani and Megan walked inside and made their way to the reception desk for the indoor firing range. As a member, Megan had already completed the necessary paperwork, but Dani was asked to sign a waiver and present identification. She decided to rent a gun so she could shoot as well, choosing the same model Megan had bought, minus the pink pearl handle.

"Are you two sisters?" the man behind the counter asked.

Dani and Megan looked at each other, each trying hard not to roll their eyes. They used to get this all the time in high school. Even though Megan had blue eyes and Dani's were brown, they were nearly the same height, both with long dark hair. "We're not, but people ask us that all the time."

"We might as well be sisters," Megan said. "We tell each other everything."

The man behind the counter simply nodded. "You're free to go through the airlock. You have lanes five and six."

They put on their ear and eye protection and headed in. There was only one other person in the range and it appeared as though they were packing up. Dani got settled in her lane, arranging her ammunition to one side, placing the gun on the ledge pointing downrange and carefully loading the magazine just as her father had taught her years ago. As a police officer, he'd been thorough about gun safety, drilling it into her head. She'd found it a bit annoying as a teenager, but she could appreciate it now.

Both women sent their targets downrange and began shooting. Dani was impressed with this little gun. It fit perfectly into her hand and had very little kickback. She had to admit that she was proud of her aim, too. She hadn't lost it after all these years. Between reloads, she watched to see how Megan was doing. Shot after shot, she hit close to dead center of the target, the usual outline of a faceless man. Wherever Richard Lowell was lurking these days, he'd better give her a wide berth.

Dani used up her practice ammunition and stood back, watching Megan as she kept going. She waited for Megan to quit, or even just notice her, but she didn't. She kept reloading round after round. Megan's shoulders were tense. Her jaw was set with determination. After about ten minutes of this, Dani noticed that Megan was trembling as she went to reload. Dani stepped forward and placed a hand on her shoulder.

Megan jumped and pulled off her earmuffs. "What's wrong? Is something wrong?"

"No, honey. Everything is just fine, I hope. But if you don't slow down, you're going to cut that target clean in two."

Megan's brow was glistening with sweat. Her eyes were wild. She sucked in a deep breath and blew it from her lips. "I think I need to get out of here."

"Good idea. Let's scoot." Dani gathered her things and met Megan at the door. She turned in the gun she'd rented, and they made their way outside.

As soon as they were back in fresh air, Megan leaned over and rested her hands on her knees, like she was exhausted. "I feel like I'm losing it. Some times it feels like somebody is trying to squeeze the life out of me."

Dani again went to comfort her. "You're grieving, honey. You lost your brother. Your marriage isn't what you thought it was. Honestly, I'm surprised you're even able to get out of bed in the morning and go to work. I don't know if I could do that."

Megan straightened and held her hand to her chest, taking more deep breaths. "It's not so much what he did to me. It's Jason. My brother is gone. My sweet, amazing brother. He had his whole life ahead of him and he's gone. And my niece, Savannah, not only had to lose her mom, she's lost her daddy, as well. It's just not fair, Dani. It's not fair." The tears rolled down Megan's cheeks and Dani knew that her best friend was in agony. Megan never cried. She was always tough about everything.

"You're absolutely right. It's not fair at all."

"I would kill him if he was here. I'd just kill him. I'd shoot him dead and the police could come and cart me off and I wouldn't care."

"Let's not think about that right now. I don't want my best friend to go to jail." She took Megan's hand and led her back to the car. They both climbed in. "Cole is on the case, and I know he's determined to catch him."

Megan shook her head and stared down into her lap, picking at her fingernail. "I hope to hell he does. If he doesn't, I'm going to have to do it myself."

Dani wished at that moment that she could do something to help. Anything. Maybe keeping her distance from Cole was the best course of action. She didn't want to be a distraction. That being said, she couldn't exactly go back on her promise to bring the boys to his ranch tomorrow. They were already so excited about it.

"I think you need some closure," Dani said. "I mean, you're caught in this impossible situation— you can't even talk about Jason or Rich because of the investigation. But maybe it would be helpful if you had a small memorial for Jason. Something private where you and Aaron and Savannah can say goodbye."

Megan hung her head, the tears falling onto her lap. "You're right. Maybe I just need to say goodbye."

"I think you'll feel better. You can't keep everything bottled up inside forever. And until Rich is caught, you know that's going to be the way things have to be."

Megan sat a little straighter and dabbed at her eyes with a tissue she'd pulled from her handbag. "Maybe we could have it at Aaron's house. Savannah is living there full-time now. I don't want it to be too much of a disruption for her. She's still so little."

"I think it sounds wonderful. I'm happy to help in any way I can."

"I'd want Will to be there, too. He's been so great to me since this happened. He's the one who brought Cole on board with the investigation in the first place. I'd like to invite Cole, too, but only if it's okay with you."

Dani had to think about that for a minute. "This isn't a ploy, is it?"

"I tend to think of situations that are a bit more romantic than a memorial service if I'm trying to set up a couple." Megan looked up and flashed her trademark smile, making Dani feel one hundred times better.

"Perfect. Just name the day and I'll be there."

"I'll talk to Aaron, but I'd like to do it sooner rather than later. Maybe Saturday."

"I'll keep it open."

Megan reached for Dani's hand. "Thank you. For everything. I don't know what I would do without you."

"You're welcome, and I feel the exact same way. Now, let's go get some lunch. I'm buying."

"Cocktails, too?"

Dani turned on the ignition and shifted the car into gear. "Of course. I think we both could use one."

Five

Cole didn't get a wink of sleep on Wednesday night. Between the investigation, the upcoming sting operation and knowing Dani and the boys were coming to the ranch, there was too much rattling around in his head.

The topic that really wouldn't go away, no matter how hard he tried to focus on other things, was that of Colin and Cameron. Could they be his sons? The fact that he couldn't let it go when he had so much on his professional plate said a lot. Cole was frequently guilty of putting career before anything else. He just couldn't walk away from the immense satisfaction of it. It all led back to Cole's childhood fascination with the Rangers and their ability to solve tough cases.

No matter what it was, Cole had to find the truth and get to the heart of what was right.

Cole had to find out the truth about Colin and Cameron. Had he and Dani conceived twin boys? Or had Taylor Blake been not only lucky enough to have been with Dani, but to have fathered her children? He cringed at the thought, but the alternative wasn't much better. If Colin and Cameron were his sons, Dani had kept a massive secret from him for more than five years. Of course, he'd stomped on her heart, so maybe in her mind, they were even.

Cole was out in the yard talking to one of his ranch hands. He'd been working on the investigation all morning and was sorely out of the loop with the state of the ranch. One of the mares had given birth to a healthy foal that morning. The boys were in for a real treat. In the middle of their conversation, a minivan came up the driveway. Dani was in the passenger seat, and a woman Cole didn't recognize was driving. When it came to a stop, the side doors opened on their own, and the boys unbuckled their seat belts and ran up to him. Cole waved to Dani as the boys nearly tackled him in the driveway.

"Mr. Cole, we're here!" Cameron exclaimed while Colin nodded in agreement.

"Hi, guys. I'm happy to see you."

"Hey, Cole," Dani said, walking toward him. Her perfume got to him first, then the gorgeous skin of her shoulders, left bare by her white tank top. And to think he'd had his hands all over her the other night...

the very idea made his whole body come alive with electricity. "I need to ask you a favor."

"Yes. Of course." *Anything.*

"That's my nanny, Elena. She wants to check out the antiques at Priceless. I told her she could take the minivan since not much can fit in the back of my convertible. Do you think you could give us a ride home when we're done?"

"I'm happy to do it." He'd never before felt that the chance to give someone a ride was a prize, but he sure felt that way right now.

"Great. As long as you don't get any ideas about what this means. We're just in need of a ride. That's it."

Cole fought the sigh that wanted to leave his lips. "Don't worry. You'll get no ideas from me."

"Good. Thank you. I appreciate it. Let me get their boosters." Dani headed over to the minivan, where Elena was a step ahead, pulling out the boys' car seats. Dani waved goodbye to Elena, who drove off a moment later.

"What do you boys want to see first?" Cole asked.

"Horses!" Cameron didn't hesitate with his answer.

"How about you, Colin?" Cole asked.

"That sounds fun. As long as it's okay with you."

Cole arched his eyebrows at Dani and put on his sunglasses. "Horses it is."

The boys tore off, Cameron leading the way down to the stables.

"I noticed you can tell the boys apart." Dani was right at his side as they strolled along.

"It's more from the way they talk than their appearance. Colin hangs back a little bit. Cameron's more outgoing."

"Ever the detective, huh? Always observing."

"I couldn't stop if I wanted to." What he really wanted to say was that Colin looked and acted a lot like him—same faint freckles, same need to observe before speaking. But again, he had to wonder if his mind was playing tricks on him, if this was all just projection because a part of him wanted a connection to Dani. Even if they couldn't be together as a couple, perhaps they could be close again. As intense and passionate as their relationship had once been, they'd always been great friends. He'd have been lying if he'd said he didn't want at least that much again.

When they got to the barn, Cole quietly let Colin and Cameron know what was in store. "Boys, we have a brand-new foal in the barn. A baby horse. She was just born this morning, so we have to be real quiet around her. We don't want to spook her or her mama, okay?"

"Can you do that?" Dani asked.

Mouths zipped tight, both boys nodded in agreement, their eyes wide as saucers. Cole adored their sweet innocence. It was such a wonderful change of pace from the usual things he dealt with—grueling ranch work and chasing evil men.

"Okay, then. Let's go." Cole led them over to the

far end of the barn. One of the ranch hands was watching closely, arms resting on the gate to the stall. Cole realized then that they'd have to pick up the boys for them to see. He wanted to give Peanut and her new baby all the privacy they deserved.

Dani scooped up Cameron, and with a nod, let Cole know it was okay for him to do the same with Colin. Cole held on tight to the boy, struggling a bit with how to best hold him. He didn't want to drop him. Dani demonstrated, putting Cameron on her hip. Cole followed her lead, and that made things much better. They crept toward the stall and there was the mama horse, eating away while the foal suckled. The boys were both completely still and silent, just watching. Peanut pulled away from her food and let out a blow, probably curious about her visitors. The foal unlatched from the teat and took a few unsteady steps around the stall, shaking and hobbling. Cole watched in awe, just as he had a hundred times before. This was one of Cole's favorite parts of being a rancher—new life. He loved it when the animals gave birth and there were babies around to care for.

"Wow," Colin whispered right into Cole's ear. "She can walk already?"

Cole grinned. "She can."

Dani and Cole put the boys back down on the ground and led them out of the barn. As soon as they were out of earshot of Peanut, the boys were full of questions.

"Why was the baby sucking on the mama's belly?" Cameron asked.

"That's where she gets the milk," Cole answered.

"I don't understand how a horse can walk right after being born. Doesn't she need to learn how to do that?" Colin asked.

Cole was ready to give him the nickname of Mr. Professor. "They're just born knowing how to do it. Pretty cool, huh?"

"I've seen pictures of us when we were first born, and we were very small and wrapped up in blankets. I don't think we were able to do much more than cry," Colin said.

Cole swallowed hard as that picture popped up in his head. If these were his boys, he'd missed out on a lot. First steps, first words and—certainly from Colin—first questions. At some point, he was going to have to just come out and ask Dani the hard question, but not in front of the boys. It wasn't right. And if he was being honest with himself, the answer scared him. If she'd kept this from him, she'd had her reasons. Dani didn't do anything without good cause.

"Would you boys like to get up on a horse? Go for a ride around the pen?" Cole asked.

"Yes, please," Cameron said.

"Just nothing dangerous, please," Dani interjected.

"I promise they'll get nothing but the oldest, kindest horse. That would be Gentry. She's out in the pasture right now, but she'll come if I whistle. We'll have to get her saddled up, but she loves kids."

They strolled out past the barn to a small pasture for the horses. The longhorns were kept farther away from the main house. Gentry was easily found with her chestnut-and-white coloring. She was a pretty horse now, but she'd been stunning in her prime.

Cole placed his thumb and middle finger between his lips and whistled. Gentry looked up and, seeming resigned, made her way to the gate. Cole unhooked the latch and started to walk right up to her, but the boys and Dani hung back. "It's okay, boys. Come on. She won't hurt you."

Cameron sprinted into action, and Colin followed. Gentry dropped her head when she got close to Cole and he gave her exactly what she wanted—scratches behind both ears.

Cole took the boys and Gentry down to the small corral next to the barn, saddled up the horse and let them take turns riding her. They took to it easily. These boys were born ranchers—one more reason for him to wonder if they might be his. Dani leaned against the fence, her long hair flowing over her shoulder in the breeze. She kept watch over her boys, but Cole also caught her keeping an eye on him once or twice. When that happened, their gazes locked for a heartbeat or two, making Cole's pulse thunder in his ears. Then Dani would drop her head or look away, and he'd be plunged right back into self-doubt.

He tried not to think too much about the tension between them, the unfinished business, but it was next to impossible. It was all around him. An indelible force. He'd love it if she'd let down her guard and talk to him about the boys. But how could he expect her to open up about anything when it was his secret that kept them apart in the first place? Especially since his was a secret he refused to share. He didn't want anyone's pity because of the tumor.

Just then a familiar, gleaming RV pulled up in front of the house. Cole's stomach sank. His parents. Those two and Dani did not have a good history. If he was trying to smooth things over with her, his mom and dad were going to stand in the way. No question about that.

"Come on, boys, we're going to let Gentry have a rest," Cole said. He waved over one of the ranch hands to have him take care of the horse.

"We were having fun," Cameron said, seeming disappointed.

Dani strolled over. "Who's that in the big RV?"

It wasn't merely big, it was massive. A top-of-the-line Prevost, with a king-size bed in the master suite, hardwood floors, and marble tables. His parents had spared no expense. Cole smiled, as if that was going to make this any easier. "That would be my parents."

"Your parents are here?" Dani muttered with a biting edge to her voice. "Why didn't you tell me they were coming over?"

Cole was already on edge. His parents had not been particularly kind to Dani when he and Dani were together. "I didn't know they were going to. They're retired now and living out of that thing most of the year." He pointed in the direction of the RV, just as his parents climbed out. Of course, they managed to spot Cole, Dani and the boys right away. "But they drop in unannounced every now and then to check in on things with the ranch. I'm so sorry. I know they're not your favorite people."

"Great. And I have no car. I really don't think this is a good idea."

Cole couldn't help but notice the panic in Dani's voice. This was a big deal for her. "Don't worry. I won't let anything bad happen." If only he could be so certain that he could keep that promise.

"I swear to God, Cole. If they say one thing to me, I'm leaving. I will call Elena and get her to pick us up."

Cole rested his hand on her shoulder, trying to ignore how good it felt to have his fingers on her bare skin. "I will drive you myself if something happens. Or better yet, I'll tell them to leave. Just give them a chance, Dani. They've both mellowed out a bit with retirement."

Dani pressed her lips together tightly. "Hmm." She did not seem convinced.

"Come on. Let's just say hello." The four of them made the trek up to the driveway. Cole's mom, Bonnie, approached them, her curly blond hair up in a ponytail. Always impeccably dressed, she was wearing a sleeveless black blouse and white Capris, her trademark diamond stud earrings glinting in the sunlight. Mom spread her arms wide, but to Cole's great surprise, that embrace was not meant for him—it was for Dani.

"Dani Moore. I can't believe you're here. It's so nice to see you." She gave Dani a pat on the back and stepped back. "You look just as gorgeous as always." She turned to Cole's dad. "Gus, doesn't she look amazing?"

"She does. She does." Dad was looking especially tan, and dressed like he was ready to go golfing, in khakis and a blue polo. Now that he was retired, he always looked more at ease than he had when he was still running the ranch. He hugged Dani, too, then shook Cole's hand. "Son. Good to see you."

"Nice to see you guys. I wish I would've known you were coming." *Seriously. Maybe give a guy a phone call next time?*

"And who do we have here?" Cole's mom asked.

Colin and Cameron introduced themselves. Cole was impressed.

"Would you boys like some cookies? And to check out our RV? If it's okay with your mother, of course."

Dani crossed her arms. "Oh, sure. Go right ahead."

As soon as his parents walked off with the boys, Cole had to check in and see how Dani was feeling. "That wasn't so bad. I mean, considering how you feel about them."

"Anything I feel about them is because of things that they said. I never wanted anything but to be accepted, Cole."

"I talked to them about it that one time, and they got better, didn't they?"

"And then the accident happened and it got ugly.

You weren't there in that hospital waiting room. It was awful."

Cole sighed. Everything came back to the accident. "I'm so sorry. I don't know what to say. If I had been there, I would've told them to stop. I would've told them it wasn't right."

Dani shrugged and looked off in the distance, shaking her head. "I guess I just need to get over it, but it's hard."

"I understand. I'd appreciate your willingness to put up with them for a little while today."

"I'll do my best." She started to walk toward the RV. "Plus, there's no way I'm getting the boys out of here until they've had a chance to swim in your pool."

After spending several hours with Cole's parents, anybody could've knocked Dani over with a feather. Bonnie and Gus hadn't just been nice or pleasant. They'd gone out of their way to be kind. Dani almost asked Cole if his parents had been abducted by aliens.

They'd spent a few hours sitting out by the pool while Cole swam with the boys. Cole had bought the fixings for sandwiches and a fruit salad for lunch, and Bonnie not only deferred to Dani's expertise in the kitchen, she applauded it, declaring the herb aioli she made "divine." Now that it was getting to be late afternoon, Dani was ready to head home. The boys were tired and she was, too, even though she'd had an incredible day.

"Cole, do you mind taking the boys and me home?"

Cole hopped up from the couch, where he was sitting with the boys and his dad. "Yeah. Absolutely. I'll grab my keys."

Bonnie pulled Dani aside. "It was really nice to see you today, Dani. I just want to tell you that I'm sorry for the way I acted with you when you and Cole were together. And especially for the things I said after the accident." She placed her hand on Dani's shoulder. "I hope that maybe now that you're a mom you can understand a bit of what makes you feel protective. That's all it was. Me going overboard with being a mama bear. I'm not proud of it. And I do regret it. Please accept my apology."

Dani could hardly believe what she was saying. And, she had to admit, she did understand what Bonnie was saying. She had her hyperprotective moments, too. "Thank you, Bonnie. I appreciate that. I really do."

"Now that you're back in town, I hope that you and Cole can spend some more time together."

"We'll see. We're getting reacquainted right now." Dani didn't want to say any more.

"Ready?" Cole asked.

"Yeah. I think the boys already ran outside."

"Of course they did."

Cole got the boys, the booster seats and everything else loaded into the truck, and off they went to Dani's house. Despite their busy day, the boys were a flurry of conversation. Cole stayed quiet, so Dani did, too. She needed time to think about today. She'd had a good time, even with his parents, which she had not thought was possible. And to think, just that morning she'd been dreading seeing Cole. She still didn't like the way she behaved around him, acting as if she had no common sense. She didn't like that he still had that kind of control over her, whether he realized it or not.

When they got to the house, Cole asked if he could come in and see her new place. It was against Dani's better judgment, but it was so hard to say no to Cole, especially after he'd gone out of his way to make their day so special.

Of course, once the boys realized Cole was coming in, they weren't about to let him leave.

"Can he stay for story time?" Cameron asked.

Dani had very little resolve at this point. "Sure. But you both need a bath first. I don't care how much time you spent in that pool, you're both filthy."

Just then, Cole received a phone call from one of the FBI agents, and excused himself, walking into the kitchen. He'd gone for hours without working, so that was no big surprise. He was front and center for story time, though, listening to Dani read one of the boys' favorite books about trains that could talk. She glanced over at him at one point while she was reading and couldn't help but notice the way the boys wanted to be near him. It created the strangest feeling in her chest—both happy and sad. That was the way things should've been. The way they could've been.

"Can Mr. Cole read us a book now?"

Dani wasn't sure she could take any more sweet

and tender moments between the boys and Cole. It was too strong a reminder of how the life they could've had together never materialized.

"Maybe some other time, honey. It's late. You both need to get some sleep."

Dani closed the door on the boys' room after tucking them in. Cole was still by her side. It had been the most incredible day—the horses, the time spent laughing in his kitchen and watching the boys swim in Cole's enormous, over-the-top pool. She'd certainly had her pangs of guilt over not telling him about the boys all these years, but that was a scenario of Cole's design. She'd never wanted to break up. She hadn't wanted to leave Royal, that was for sure.

"Heading home?" Dani half hoped he wasn't, even when she knew what a bad idea it was for him to stay. She had so little willpower when it came to him.

"I'd love a glass of wine if you're offering."

She owed him that much for such a wonderful day. "Absolutely. Let's go downstairs." They descended her sweeping staircase and trailed into the kitchen, where Dani pulled out a bottle of cabernet and opened it. She sniffed the cork and handed it to Cole. Working at the Glass House gave her access to some incredible wines, most of which were private reserve and difficult to find.

He took a whiff and shrugged. "Smells like wine to me."

"You are a true connoisseur."

He winked and tossed the cork in the trash. Dani didn't want to admit it, but she liked that he was so comfortable in her house already. He looked good here. Too good. Good enough that all she wanted was for him to take his shirt off. How could she have let herself forget until the other night exactly how much she loved his chest and shoulders? She would've been lying if she said that she didn't long to touch him again, to have him pressed up against her. Being this close to him was only making her lips twitch with the memory of his kiss.

Cole raised his glass and clinked it against Dani's. "To a great day."

"To a great day." Dani sipped her wine, trying to keep her eyes off Cole, but it was impossible. Part of it was just general admiration. He'd been in the sun most of the day and had that glow that took her breath away. The way it played off his icy blue eyes just wasn't fair. No woman should have to withstand the pressure of being in the same room with that, knowing that it was best if she walked away. It was so impossible it should be an Olympic event. *And now, with the bronze medal in Resisting Cole Sullivan, is Danica Moore of the USA. She could've taken the silver if she hadn't allowed him to kiss her the other night and let it snowball from there.*

Cole was staring off into space, absentmindedly gnawing on his lower lip, which was ridiculously sexy.

"You seem preoccupied. Everything okay?" Was he thinking what she was? That a kiss might be a bad idea, but a whole lot of fun?

"I'm fine. I was just so distracted by you and the

boys today that I stopped thinking about the investigation into Jason's murder. Now that things have quieted down, I guess my mind naturally wants to go there."

"I'm sure it's hard to keep your mind off it. Spending time with Megan yesterday really put everything into perspective. She's struggling. She's sad and mad and I think she's even a little scared, not knowing what Rich might do."

"I know. The whole thing is a nightmare, especially for her." The crease between his eyebrows got deeper. Dani knew that meant he was stressed. "After spending time with the boys today, I realize just how much this is going to impact Jason's daughter, Savannah. She's not that much older than them."

"What's the next step? With the investigation?"

"You know I shouldn't talk about it."

"I know, but it's my best friend we're talking about. And you know you can trust me to keep my lips shut. I know exactly how dangerous things can get if someone goes around flapping their mouth." Dani's dad had worked in law enforcement. She knew not to talk.

"I'm coordinating a sting in the Sierra Nevadas near the location where the plane carrying Jason and Rich went down. There's a sheriff up there who is a real slimeball. Everybody says he's crooked, but nobody's caught him. We got a tip that he took a bribe to lie about who died in that plane crash and have the body cremated before anyone could identify it."

"That's horrible. Did you say the Sierra Nevadas? Whereabouts?"

"Durango City. It's a real mess. The sheriff is pretty slick, but we're worried about him getting skittish. He doesn't trust anyone. And it's my job to figure out how we get him to confess on tape to everything that happened."

Dani couldn't believe what she was hearing. "What's this sheriff's name?"

"Billy Orson. Real son of a bitch."

She'd heard Cole correctly. The sound of that name made the hair on the back of her neck stand up. "I've cooked for him before. In his home."

"What? Are you serious?" Cole set down his wineglass.

"Yes. Remember when I got my first job out of culinary school working for that catering company? We got hired by the sheriff to cater this very extravagant party he threw. I guess he had the hots for my boss. They'd met in Vegas on vacation. As near as I could tell, he was just trying to get her into bed."

"And what happened?"

"We were flown out there. Just the two of us. I was the sous-chef. He hired servers, but we did all of the food. I remember thinking that it made no sense that a sheriff would have a house that big and fancy. And he paid for us to fly out there, first class. Anyway, he was a total creep. Kept hitting on me all night."

"Do you think he would recognize you?"

"Probably not. It was seven years ago. My hair was shorter and much lighter."

"Do you remember the house well?"

"Yeah. We spent an entire day there and stayed overnight."

Cole leaned against the kitchen counter, rubbing his forehead.

"Are you okay?"

He looked up at her, nearly knocking her over with the intensity in his eyes. "Yeah. Just got a lot of stupid ideas going through my head."

"Like what?"

He straightened and waved it off, stuffing his hands into his back pockets. "It's crazy."

"Just tell me." She topped off her glass and his, as well. Judging by the tone of Cole's voice, they both might need it.

"So I'm running a sting to catch the sheriff. I got myself a spot at a cocktail party he's hosting to court investors in a pipeline project up in the mountains. I'll be posing as a hotshot money guy from Houston. But one of the FBI agents helping us on the case is convinced I won't be able to get him to confess anything. She says I need a woman with me."

Dani put two and two together so fast her head was spinning. This was perfect. She could finally help Megan in some real way. And all she had to do was go to a cocktail party and talk to an overly flirtatious scumbag? She'd done that so many times in her life, she could practically do it in her sleep.

But she also had to think about the boys. "Are we

talking a dangerous situation? I mean, it's a cocktail party. How dangerous could it possibly be?"

"The FBI will be on-site that night. So not super dangerous. But still." He pressed his lips together and looked right at her, shaking his head. "I know what you're thinking, Dani. What about the boys?"

"Precisely why I asked if it was going to be dangerous. I know the house. That's got to count for something, doesn't it?"

"It does. Still doesn't mean I think it's our best shot. I need a woman who can persuade him to talk."

"Like a woman who's been around law enforcement her whole life? A woman who is smart and, most important, knows how this guy operates? I am not afraid of him. If he was standing in front of me right now, I know I could get him to talk."

Cole drew a breath through his nose. "I'll think about it. And I'll talk to Agent Stanton about it. See what she says."

Dani had to admit she was a bit disappointed. "Okay. I understand if I might not be the right person to do it."

A quiet laugh left Cole's lips. She loved that sound. She loved hearing it in the middle of the night, his mouth near her ear, his body warm against her. "You're perfect for this. You're beautiful and smart and sexy. What more could I possibly want?"

"I don't know, Cole. What more could you want?" She hated the way her voice cracked, but this was clawing at the essence of what had hurt most about their breakup. She hadn't been enough for him. And she still didn't understand why.

"Nothing. Nothing at all."

She wasn't sure if they were talking about the investigation or their past, but she had to make her case one more time. "Then let me go to this party with you. Let me help you get some justice for a little girl who doesn't have her daddy anymore."

That idea really hit home with her. Her dad had protected her so fiercely when she was growing up, buffering her from her troubled mother. It nearly killed Dani when that was all taken away from her. She hated the thought that Savannah was having to go through the same thing.

"I promise I will think about it." He reached out for her shoulder. His touch brought up every conflicted feeling, her heart and her body at war with each other. "You're so amazing for even offering to do it. Thank you." He squeezed her bare shoulder then trailed his fingers down the back of her arm. His touch was impossibly light, but there was no mistaking what it was saying. It left a white-hot path in its wake, warming Dani's face and chest. "I'm only considering it because I would die before I let anyone so much as lay a hand on you. I would never let anything bad happen to you. Never."

"That's good to know." Cole did not throw those words around lightly, but the reality of their past was that he had not only let something bad happen to her, he'd done it. "It's getting late."

"It's been a long day. We're both tired." He nestled his fingers in the palm of her hand, then began to journey back up the length of her arm. He stepped closer to her, until they were toe-to-toe. He dropped his head. At that scant distance, it made his shoulders that much more deliciously imposing. She watched as his chest rose and fell with every breath, hypnotizing her with its steady rhythm.

She couldn't help the way she was drawn to him. When his hand reached the tender underside of her upper arm and his fingertips grazed the side of her breast, she sucked in a sharp breath. She dared to look up into his face, just as a self-satisfied smile crossed his lips.

"I'd forgotten how much I love it when you make that noise."

Before Dani knew what was happening, she was kissing him, if only to get him to not talk about her weakness for him. She flattened a hand against his solid chest, curling her fingers to feel the flex of his muscles, while her other hand grabbed his neck and tugged him in closer. Taking what she wanted was so liberating, she didn't know which way was up. His arms snaked around her waist, his hands smoothing over the small of her back and trailing down until he squeezed her bottom. Dani bowed into him. Memories of the other night swirled in her consciousness. Had it really felt that good to take off his clothes, or was she making too much of it because she wanted to end the longest drought of her adult life? Maybe this required further investigation.

Cole angled his head and took the kiss even

deeper. He'd always known how to make her feel desired. "I want you, Dani," Cole muttered between kisses. As if his words weren't quite enough, he grabbed her thigh and hitched her leg up on his hip.

"I want you, too." She couldn't lie. She pressed her center against his hipbone, creating heat and friction that left her dizzy.

They kissed again, Cole's lips so firm and insistent, his tongue quickly seeking hers. He cupped her breast with his hand, brushing against her nipple with his thumb. Through the thin cotton of her dress and her silky bra, it was almost as good as if he'd touched her skin. But she wanted more. She wanted the real thing.

She pulled the strap of her dress off her shoulder, and tugged down the front of her dress. "Touch me, Cole. Please." She was breathless, her chest heaving.

Cole looked at her, slack-jawed and his eyes heavy with lust. She could see his internal struggle, the way his eyes stormed. She would've been mad at his hesitancy if she hadn't endured so much of it herself the other night at his house.

"I want to Dani. I do. But maybe you were right the other night. Maybe it's a mistake if you and I give in to this."

The reality of her situation slammed into her. Where would she be after a casual tryst with Cole? It would be that much harder to stay away from him. Once she had a real taste of him, she knew she'd only want more. And she had other people to worry about—Cameron and Colin, to be exact. She sighed heavily. "I understand. It was a great day, but you should probably go."

Cole gently let her leg go and stepped back. He drew in a deep breath through his nose and neatened his hair with his hand. "Okay, then."

"Sorry." It had to be physically difficult for him, but she was just as raring to go as he was.

"Don't apologize, Dani. It was my idea." Cole snapped up his keys from the kitchen counter. "I don't think my ego can take you calling me a mistake again."

Six

Dani's biggest worry about Jason's memorial was how Megan was going to handle it. After their time at the firing range the other day, Dani knew pretty well how much all of this was eating her up inside. But she also knew that Megan needed today. She couldn't move forward with her life until she said goodbye to her brother, as sad as that was.

Cole had called that morning and asked if Dani wanted a ride, and Dani had said yes, mostly because she still felt bad about the way things had ended the other night. He'd put a stop to things, but he'd made it clear it was because of the precedent she'd set with that word—*mistake*. It didn't mean that she hadn't gone to sleep that night, immensely frustrated, thinking about how Cole could've been in her bed, weighing her down with his solid frame and sending to her peak over and over again.

He picked her up at her house, and Dani hurried outside as soon as he arrived.

"I was hoping to see the boys today," Cole said. The disappointment in his voice was heavy, which worried Dani. Did he suspect they were his? She shuttered aside her paranoia by focusing instead on how incredibly hot he looked in a charcoal-gray suit and his black Stetson.

"Oh. I'm sorry. Elena took them to see Aunt Dot." Cole was getting attached to them and she knew they were getting attached to him. It was dangerous territory that made her wonder about the wisdom of spending more time with him. Still, looking at his face and his soft and tender eyes, she couldn't deny that there was this pull deep inside her that made her want to be with him.

"Okay then. I guess I'll see them some other time."

Dani got settled in the truck and decided she should change the subject. "You're looking sharp, Sullivan."

He smiled and pulled out of the driveway. "Thanks. You aren't looking too shabby yourself. Although I like seeing you in brighter colors. Like red." He cleared his throat and cast a quick glance at her.

"Yeah. I noticed."

"Can you blame me?"

Dani just stared out the window, not knowing how to answer. She'd known exactly what she was doing when she went to his house that night. There was just some part of her that wasn't willing to admit it. At least not out loud.

"Are you going to respond?" Will asked.

"I don't know what you want me to say, Cole. Did I wear the dress to get your attention? Yes. Absolutely. Did I wear it so you would kiss me? No. That was not the point."

"Then what was the point?" Cole took the turn into Aaron's neighborhood.

Dani looked down at her hands, which were folded neatly in her lap. Could she own up to this? Now seemed as good a time as any. "I wanted you to see what you were missing."

"Well, mission accomplished."

Dani was ready to put this subject to rest. She had nothing else to add, and she'd already come clean. "Is Will going to be there today?"

"I'm sure he will be. He and Megan have been spending so much time together."

"They're in such a weird predicament. Technically still married, needing to pretend like everything is fine."

"Definitely makes for a situation only the two of them can understand."

Dani sighed, just thinking about Megan's lot in life. "I'm glad we're doing this. I think it will be good for everyone."

"It was sweet of you to suggest it." Cole pulled into the driveway on Aaron Phillips's impressive estate and stopped before the brick mansion standing sentry on the manicured grounds.

They made their way to the grand arched front door, greeted by Kasey Monroe, Aaron's executive assistant turned nanny, and now, his fiancé. "Thanks you two for coming. Everyone is out back. Savannah is chasing the puppies so she can put them in the mudroom."

Cole and Dani walked inside. Savannah was indeed running around with one dog tucked under her arm and in hot pursuit of the other, all while wearing a lavender dress with a full skirt and Mary Janes.

"Does she need help?" Cole asked.

"No. She's the dog whisperer. I just try to not get mad when they eat my shoes."

They followed Kasey out to the backyard, which was just as stunning as the one at Cole's house. "Megan, Will and Aaron are over by the koi pond under the tree. We're going to do everything over there. I'll go get Savannah."

Dani and Cole wound their way past the pool to the serene setting.

Megan pulled Dani into a hug right away. "I'm so glad you're here."

"Of course. You know I wouldn't miss this for anything."

"You, too, Cole," Megan added. "It means a lot that you came. I know it was important to Will that you were here."

Dani looked over at Will and Aaron, who were immersed in what appeared to be an intense conversation. That was the nature of Aaron, though. Everything about him was strong and at full force.

Kasey appeared, holding Savannah's hand. Savannah was really starting to shoot up. It wouldn't be long until the little girl was as tall as Kasey. "I think we're all ready. The puppies have been secured."

Aaron and Will broke up their conversation and acknowledged Cole and Dani with a nod. Aaron stepped closer to Megan and whispered in her ear before scooping Savannah up into his massive arms and taking a spot right next to Kasey.

Megan removed her sunglasses and made eye contact with everyone in attendance. "Aaron and I have asked Will to deliver the eulogy today." She cast an adoring look at Aaron. "My brother and I aren't quite ready to talk about it yet. We just want the chance to honor Jason and the life he shared with us."

Megan stepped back and made room for Will to stand in front of the koi pond. The sunshine filtered through the leaves of the trees overhead, casting beautiful dappled light onto the stone patio.

Will cleared his throat, and Dani could see the pain in his eyes. "We're here today to honor the life of Jason Phillips, a brother, a father and an incredible friend. I will keep this short, because I know that words won't bring him back. I didn't write any of this down, but Jason always spoke from the heart, and I want to do the same for him." Will stood a little straighter. "This has been hard for all of us. The loss we have experienced is great. But we still have today. And we still have each other. Jason would've wanted us to cling to what we have, not think about what we have lost."

Will looked at each one of them. "What's keeping me going right now is being able to see Savannah, Aaron and Megan. I see Jason in all of you. Aaron, I see your brother's strength and intensity. That tenacity has shown in the investigation into his death. You uncovered details that have helped Cole and the entire team."

Aaron's jaw quivered, and Kasey leaned in to him.

"Savannah, I look at you, and I see the hope and youthful spirit that your dad always had. He and I were only a little older than you when we met. I will never forget that day." Will's voice faltered, in a way that made Dani wonder if he could continue, but he collected himself. "We were the very best of friends. We both loved horses, and we loved living in Texas. We'd get in some trouble from time to time. But your dad wasn't afraid to admit it if he'd made a mistake. That's an important life lesson. You have to own your mistakes and move on."

Dani swallowed hard and looked over at Cole. Had she made a mistake with keeping the boys from him? She'd been so certain when she was in New York that she hadn't, but as she spent more and more time with him, that certainty was giving way to questions.

Will turned to Megan and reached out for her hand. "Megan…"

"Don't you dare make me cry, Will," Megan said.

"I did not put on waterproof mascara today." Everyone laughed quietly.

He stepped closer to her and put his arm around her shoulders. "It's okay to cry. It only means that you loved him."

Megan looked into Will's eyes and shook her head. "I did love him. I loved him so much."

Will set a finger under her chin and kept her face tilted upward. "That love is still here, Megan. It lives inside you. I see it every time I talk to you. I see it when you laugh. Don't ever let go of that. Hold on to it forever. For Aaron. For Savannah. For me." Will broke down and pulled Megan into his arms.

Dani leaned into Cole, and he tugged her closer. The entire scene was so overwhelming, reminding Dani just how precious loved ones were. Will and Megan had lost so much because of Rich. Will had his identity stolen. Megan had a sham marriage. They had to continue living a lie until Rich was caught. But losing Jason was obviously the breaking point for both of them.

It made Dani realize how lucky she was to have Cole to lean on right now. She closed her eyes and inhaled his warm and manly scent, allowing herself to be comforted as he trailed his warm hand up and down her arm. It felt so good when he was being protective. It felt so right in his arms. He could be her rock when he wanted to be. But did he want that? Was it possible for them to work out their differences?

Megan sniffed and wrenched herself from Will's

arms. They were holding hands, still standing close. "Okay, everyone. If Jason was here, he'd tell us that this was enough sadness for one day and we should go inside, toast to him and eat."

"It's probably time to let the dogs out of the mud-room, too," Kasey added. "There's no telling what they got into."

"Free the puppies!" Savannah wiggled out of Aaron's arms and bolted inside the house.

"You okay?" Cole asked Dani, pulling her aside.

She nodded. She wasn't really okay, but she had to be for Megan. "I'm good."

Dani and Cole went inside and had a quick bite to eat and a glass of iced tea with everyone. The mood was subdued, although Savannah kept things lighter, playing with the Newfoundland puppies on the floor. Dani couldn't take her eyes off the young girl, only two years older than Colin and Cameron. Clearly, Savannah was in a good situation, living with her uncle and Kasey, who were engaged to be married. But it still made Dani's blood boil to think about what Rich had done. And for what? Money? Was any amount of money worth taking a parent away from a child? It wasn't right. In fact, it was unthinkable.

Cole leaned closer to Dani. "You sure you're okay?"

"I am. I'm just ready to get back."

"You guys taking off?" Megan had apparently heard Dani's answer.

Dani produced a sheepish smile. "We are. Is that okay? Do you need us for anything?"

Megan got up from her seat. "I'm as good as I'm going to get at this point. Thank you for suggesting this. It was nice. Now we just need to catch that bastard Rich. I need to put this all behind me."

Dani hugged Megan, and they said their goodbyes, but Dani was haunted by what her best friend had said. *I need to put this all behind me.*

"Ready?" Cole asked after Megan walked away.

"Yes. I'm wiped out," Dani said.

"Me, too." This small gathering for Jason made Cole's charge feel all the more urgent. He had to get this case resolved as quickly as possible. Everyone had suffered too much at the hands of Rich, and every day that went by was another chance for Rich to get away.

They headed into the foyer. Will was on the phone. He held up his finger, presumably to asking them to wait.

"Well, Case, don't worry too much about me," Will said. He had to be speaking to TCC president, Case Baxter. "I've just been busy with work. You know how it goes. I appreciate the call, though. Thanks." He hung up his phone and cast Cole a look. "That was Case Baxter asking if I was okay. He said I seemed out of sorts when he saw me leaving my office at the TCC. Less than an hour ago."

The blood in Cole's veins went to ice. "Rich."

"It has to be."

Dani covered her mouth. "Oh my God."

"You didn't tip Case off that it might be Rich, did you?"

Will shook his head. "No. I think I covered pretty well."

"Good. I guess I'm glad that he's still around, because that means his stash is likely still somewhere in the county. We just need to find it. That's the key to catching him. And I need to get my hands on the security tape from the TCC. Maybe it'll tell me something about what he's up to."

"Do you think I should tell Megan?" Will asked.

Cole thought on that. Sheriff Battle had a deputy regularly patrolling her street, making sure she was safe. Plus, Megan was so independent and pissed off, knowing her, she'd probably go looking for Rich herself. "Let's keep this between us for now."

Will nodded, seeming distracted. "I don't like knowing that Rich is around. I worry for Megan's safety." He looked off toward the other room. "I just want to protect her."

"Of course you do," Dani said. "You said some lovely things about Jason today. I know it meant a lot to her."

"It's literally the least I can do," Will said. "I'm sure you've struggled with wanting to help, too."

Dani nodded. "I absolutely know what you mean."

Cole could see how much this was weighing on Will. "Okay, buddy. I'll catch up with you tomorrow, okay? And don't worry. We'll get him. I promise."

"I know we will. I know."

Dani and Cole said their goodbyes and headed

outside. Cole was trying to tamp down his frustration over not having caught Rich yet. He really wanted to think about something fun like spending time with Dani, although he was fairly sure she'd turn him down. After all, he'd been the one to stop things the other night.

"Cole." Dani stopped with a hand on his shoulder just as they got to the car. "Slow down a second. You're walking a million miles a minute."

"I am?"

She cocked both eyebrows at him. "You are. Which means that you're just as worked up about all this as I am."

"Well, of course I'm worked up about it. This case means a lot to a lot of people."

"It does. Including my best friend. Megan needs justice, Cole. You have to let me do it. You have to let me go with you on the sting."

"Dani, we've talked about this. I'm not sure it's a good idea." He turned and rounded to his side of the car.

Dani climbed inside. "Just hear me out. After sitting in that room and thinking about how much Jason is missed, seeing that little girl and knowing she doesn't have her daddy anymore? You know I lost my dad. No girl should have to grow up without a father. It's not right."

"I hear what you're saying, but I'm still not sure."

"Look. You know me. I am cool as a cucumber under pressure. And going to a party and trying to lure a man into saying something he shouldn't? I'm practically built for this job. I'm very good at getting men to do things they shouldn't."

Cole laughed quietly. "Yes. I'm aware of your superpower."

"And I know you'd never let anything happen to me." She took his hand. That one touch sent a jolt of electricity right through him.

"Is now the part where you get a man to do something he shouldn't?"

Dani smiled, which only made him do the same. He couldn't help it. "I don't know. You tell me."

She was right. She was perfect for this job. And in theory, it was a simple one. Plus, he knew Bird and Stanton. They would never let anything happen to a civilian. Even more so, he would never let anything happen to Dani. He would stand in front of a barrage of bullets for her. He did want the chance to live up to his promises to her. He knew he'd let her down all those years ago. "I won't let anything happen to you. I promise."

"Is that a yes?" Her voice was bubbly and excited.

"Yes. That's a yes."

She clapped her hands and rubbed them together. "Awesome. Tell me everything I need to know."

Cole started the car. It felt good to know she still had confidence in him. "We leave Tuesday afternoon. I have a private plane chartered."

"Fancy. Is that really necessary?"

"Yes. Sheriff Orson knows everything that happens within a hundred-mile radius of his county. He thinks I'm a major big hitter. He has to know that we're flying into that tiny airstrip in our own plane."

"Will he be able to trace where the plane came from?"

"The FBI is taking care of that. They've set up a false identity for me, and the plane is registered to that name."

"Sounds like you have it all figured out. What else is left to do before we go?"

Cole and the FBI had indeed gone over every contingency. He certainly felt prepared. Still, he'd have to be at the absolute top of his game. There was no room for mistakes. "I'll brief you on everything on the plane. But we are going to have to go dress shopping. You'll need something suitable for catching the eye of a very bad man."

"I have dresses. No need to go shopping. I attended several black-tie events in New York."

"Well, then, maybe we just need to go through your closet." Visions of Dani filling out slinky dresses popped into his head—the pleasing contours of her hips, the swell of her breasts, the sexy bow of her lower back as it led to her butt. His body was buzzing just thinking about it.

"You don't trust me to pick out my own dress?"

He did trust her to choose a gown, absolutely. Still didn't mean he didn't want to be there for it. "I need to make sure that it passes muster on the sexy scale. It needs to be really sexy."

"How sexy?" Dani's voice was soft and husky.

"Super sexy." Cole glanced at Dani just as she ran

her tongue over her plump lower lip. Cole thought he might fall over.

"We could go look now if you want. Elena won't be back with the boys for a few hours."

"So that big, beautiful house of yours is empty right now?" A few hours…the idea was exhilarating. It was terrifying, too. They'd both demonstrated their ability to stomp on the brakes when clothes started to come off. They'd both shown their hesitation with letting the other in. Trust was a funny thing, fleeting and so easily broken.

"It is. What are you implying?" The flirtation in her voice was sending electricity straight to his groin. She knew damn well what he was suggesting.

"Just want to know whether or not I'll be able to get a parking spot in your driveway. That's all."

"Oh, okay." Her voice dripped with sarcasm. She slapped his thigh with the back of her hand. "Drive the car, Sullivan. We've got dresses to pick out."

Seven

Dani glanced over at Cole as he pulled into her driveway. She loved him in jeans, but damn, the man looked good in a suit. The cut of his black jacket accentuated the strong line of his shoulders. All she wanted to do was spread her hands across his chest—under the guise of admiring what he was wearing, of course.

Cole put the car in Park and turned off the ignition. Dani's pulse couldn't settle on one speed, so it was doing crazy chaotic things in her throat right now. Cole had stated the obvious—they were about to have her big beautiful house to themselves. Did that mean they were about to put the memory of their two false starts to rest? And if so, how did she feel about that? There was so much unfinished business between them, things that had to be said, but she still wasn't sure she could trust him to truly let her in. She couldn't trust him not to hurt her again.

Inside, Dani set her purse on the kitchen counter, unsure what her next step was. "Do you want a drink?"

"I wouldn't mind a little bourbon to take the edge off. That memorial and knowing that Rich was at the TCC has my mind going about a hundred miles an hour right now."

"Sounds like a plan." Dani headed into the living room, and Cole followed. Her bar, a stunning handcrafted piece made with dark wood and glass, was in the corner near one of the front windows. Pouring the drinks, she reminded herself that she needed to keep her wits about her, but she, too, needed to soothe her ragged nerves. She was feeling jumpy and anxious, too fixated on the freedom they had right now. If he was on board, they could tear each other's clothes off right there in the living room. Maybe that was all she needed—to get Cole out of her system once and for all.

"Cheers," he said when she handed him his glass. "What are we toasting?"

"How about just that we're here, together? Nothing like a memorial service to put life into perspective."

"Hear, hear," she replied, clinking her glass with his. The bourbon went down like warm silk, leaving behind a pleasant tingle in her throat and a rush of warmth in her chest.

"Ooh. That's smooth." Cole tilted the glass and shook his head before taking another sip.

"Nothing but the best. I learned that in culinary school. It's just that I can actually afford it now."

Cole surveyed the room. "You really have done well for yourself. The house is beautiful."

"It's amazing what celebrities will pay for you to cook for them. The investments I made with the life insurance money from my father have done very well, too."

"But that's you. Standing on your own two feet. You don't need anyone else."

"I've always been that way. Never had a choice. You know that." Dani choked back the words she wanted to say. She hadn't been *exactly* like that when they had been together. She'd leaned on him, especially when she was in the stressful home stretch of culinary school. They had been a team once, and she missed that more than anything. The loss became especially apparent when she found herself with two newborns. She would've done anything to have had Cole by her side at that time. But he'd made that an impossibility.

"It's always been one of the things I admired most about you." He took the last sip of his drink and set the glass on top of the bar. His voice was as warm and smooth as the bourbon, sending ripples of recognition through Dani. She knew what that particular tone meant. He was standing only a few inches away now, his smell so sexy and inviting. "Although you have lots of things to admire." He gripped her elbow and looked down into her eyes. "Can I kiss you, Dani?"

A breathy laugh rushed past her lips. "Do you realize you have never asked me that question before?"

He was already coming in for what he'd asked for, a clever smile tugging at the corners of his enticing lips. "I never had you turn me down before the other night, either. I'm not taking any chances."

"Yes, Cole. You can kiss me."

He cupped her shoulders with his strong hands and planted a soft and sensuous, unmistakable kiss on her lips. A little tongue. Leaving her wanting more. She was dizzy from it.

"No more surprises between us, okay?" he asked.

That question was dripping with serious consequences. She sighed. Nothing between them was strictly fun and carefree, however much she wanted it to be that way, if only for an afternoon. She couldn't promise no more surprises, so she kissed him, popping up on to her tiptoes. She dug her fingers into his thick hair. He tugged her closer, giving her bottom a squeeze. Dani gasped. "Didn't you come over so we could figure out what I'm wearing to my first-ever sting operation?"

"Why do I feel like I'm being punished for stopping things the last time we kissed?"

"No punishment. Come on." Dani made her way up the stairs, Cole behind her. She was definitely aware of the sway of her own hips as she climbed those stairs. Let him get an eyeful of everything he'd been missing out on all these years.

She traipsed down the hall and into her bedroom. "Have a seat in the chair and I'll bring out a few options."

Cole marched over to the chair, but only to remove his suit coat and drape it across the back. Dani wasn't about to argue with the idea of him undressing. He sat on the bed instead, giving it a bounce. "Nice." He cocked an eyebrow at her while loosening his tie. Dani was about to be the next thing in the room to come undone.

"This will just take a minute." She retreated to her closet, mumbling to herself, "What are you doing? Do you really want to sleep with him? Won't that make things so much more complicated?"

"What was that?" Cole called from the other room. "Did you say something?"

"No. Just deciding what to show you." She rushed over to the far corner, where the full-length gowns she owned were hanging. She chose her three favorites— dark blue beaded, slinky black satin, and a red crepe mermaid gown.

She took all three dresses to Cole. "Well? Thoughts?"

He leaned back on the bed, placing his hands on the mattress and scrutinizing. "I need to see them on."

She smiled. This was definitely a fun form of seduction.

"Of course." She marched back to the closet and took off her clothes—every stitch. All three of these dresses required a strapless bra, and two required a thong or no panties at all.

She tried the blue one first. "Well?" She twirled,

loving Cole's eyes on her. All of this silky fabric against her naked body was nice, but she wished he had his hands all over her.

He bit down on his lower lip as his gazed traveled up and down her body. Her heart was thumping in anticipation. She didn't care about the dress right now. She wanted him.

"I don't think it's quite sexy enough." He shook his head. "The black one next."

Disappointed, she headed back into the closet and changed. This one was even more torturous. The soft satin skimmed her breasts as she threaded the dress over her head, causing her nipples to come to attention. Mr. Tall, Dark and Dreamy being in the other room was not helping.

"Well? Thoughts?" This time she walked right up to him, turning once and looking down at him, trying her damnedest to send him psychic messages. Even if this dress wasn't the one, it was an excellent choice for ending up in a puddle on the floor.

He reached out and touched her hip lightly. "I don't love it."

"What don't you like?" Dani looked down at herself. She loved the way this dress hugged her curves.

"I just don't think it's the one."

A frustrated grumble left her throat. "Okay, then. One more. Otherwise you're taking me shopping, and I'm telling you right now that it's not going to be cheap." She returned to the closet once more.

"Something tells me I'd live."

"Damn you, Cole Sullivan," she muttered.

"I heard you that time."

"Good." She pulled the flame-red dress from the hanger and unzipped it. It was a mermaid-style gown made of fine jersey crepe, with impossibly skinny straps and a plunging back. The skirt followed every contour of her body and then flared out at the knee, making it deliciously swishy when she walked.

She was ready for another ego-crushing comment, but this time, Cole's eyes gave it away. The smoldering flash across his face made heat plume in her chest, down her belly, and straight to her thighs. "Well?" she asked. "Thoughts?" This time she gave him no buffer, stepping so close she was between his knees. She turned slowly, letting him drink in the vision.

"Wow. Just wow."

"You're just saying that because you have a weakness for red dresses."

He shook his head. "I have a weakness for *you* in a red dress. Every other woman is on her own."

She fought a smile. Why was a compliment from Cole so much better than a kind word from another man? She had no idea. "So you approve?"

He sat straighter, bringing himself closer. His eyes were about even with her chest. "Can you move well in it?"

She leaned forward at the waist and gave him an eyeful. "I can. It's nice and stretchy. It's actually surprisingly comfortable."

He drew in a deep breath through his nose, seeming to be grappling with a few urges. Good. She'd been fighting a few of her own. He must have un-buttoned his shirt when she was in the closet the last time. There were three undone now, giving her a view of his sexy chest and the tiny patch of hair in the center of it. She wanted to tangle her fingers in it. She wanted to get lost in him.

"Good. I want you to be comfortable," he said.

"So that's that, then." She turned her back to him and cast her sights over her shoulder. "I'm going to need help with the zipper, though. It's a little sticky."

Now Cole was sitting up pin straight, his eyes plaintive. "No games, Dani."

"No games."

"Good. You knock me down a peg every time you stomp on the brakes."

Dani hated the way the past crept into these con-versations, intentional or not on either of their parts. It was omnipresent—the hurt, the transgressions, the untruths. She needed a break from all of it. She wanted to disappear into the one place she'd ever truly felt safe—Cole's arms. She wanted him to make her feel good. She wanted him to make the rest of the world go away.

Which meant she had to face this head-on. She turned and looked him square in the eye. "I brought you up to my bedroom, Sullivan. I'm trying on dresses that leave very little to the imagination, and I'm doing my best to make you want me the way I want you."

His trademark cocky smile made an appearance—the one that said the universe was particularly good at glossing over his mistakes. He was too handsome. Too likable. The irresistible golden boy, like dessert for breakfast, lunch and dinner. "You want me to show you my intentions?"

Her breath hitched in her throat. "I do."

He placed his hands on her hips, the heat from his palms nearly searing her through the dress. He curled his fingertips into her flesh and tugged her closer. Her knees were flat against the side of the mattress, his face close enough to her breasts that her nipples drew hot and tight. He trailed one hand to the small of her back and dragged the zipper down. Electricity danced along her spine as his fingertips grazed her skin along the way.

"Does this help?"

She nodded. "It does." With one hand, she slipped both dress straps from her shoulders, clutching the gown to her bosom with her other arm. "Does this help you?"

Their gazes connected. Cole's eyelids were heavy with desire, making her want to give in to this right here and now. "I want it all," he said. "Everything."

Dani let the dress drop to the floor, placed her hand on Cole's shoulder and pushed him back on the bed. She planted one knee on the mattress between his legs, unable not to notice the bulging ridge in his pants. Any doubts she'd had about whether or not he wanted her had been a waste of time and energy.

She leaned down and yanked his shirt out of the waistband of his pants, then made quick work of the buttons, traveling north as she went. As soon as his chest was bare, she stretched out along his side and let her fingers roam, threading them through the hair she'd been dying to touch mere minutes ago.

Cole rolled to his side and cupped the side of Dani's neck, his fingers warm and craving at her nape. They kissed like their lives depended on it, mouths eager and open, tongues wet and hot. Cole rolled her to her back, his thigh firmly rocking against her center, making heat flame between her legs. She couldn't remember ever wanting him more. Maybe because she knew what was in store for her and she'd gone so long without him. Too long.

"You're wearing too many clothes," she said.

He shifted to his knees and tore his shirt from his body, tossing it to the floor with her dress. She unbuckled his belt, then unhooked his pants and drew down the zipper. She could already feel the tension coming from his hips. It radiated from him like the sun off a tin roof. He pushed his trousers past his hips, leaving them bunched at his upper thighs. Dani couldn't wait anymore. She sat up and tugged down his boxer briefs and took him in her hand, stroking lightly, letting her palm roll over the smooth skin with every pass. He moaned so deeply that the bed nearly shook. Her other hand trailed down his firm belly, her fingers knowing every hard contour, remembering every luscious dip and bulge of his body.

Cole stood and shucked his remaining clothes, then climbed back onto the bed. He pulled her into his arms, kissing her softly as their legs tangled and hands roamed everywhere—hers down his back and his to her hip, then up to cup her breast. He pushed her to her back and their gazes connected as he drew delicate circles around her nipple. She felt like she was floating as the need built inside her. She loved it when he took things slow and drew out the pleasure, but there was a lot of want bubbling to the surface. She needed him.

"I'm on the pill, but do we need a condom?" She'd been in near zero danger of getting pregnant in New York, having had only one boyfriend, who hadn't lasted long. She'd only kept her prescription to regulate her cycle. Still, she knew very little about Cole's personal life while she'd been gone.

"You tell me, Dani. There's been no one since you left. No one."

She kissed him softly, to give her a second to think. "Nobody? Not a single girl you picked up at a bar or anything?"

He shook his head. "You say it like it's a bad thing."

"I just…" She searched for the right words. "I'm surprised, that's all."

"Well, do you want to be surprised, or do you want me to set your world on fire?" He pushed up on his arms, towering over her. His chest was heaving. So was hers. She hooked her leg over his hip and grabbed both of his strong shoulders.

The muscles twitched beneath her touch. "I want the fire."

As much as Cole wanted to soak up the stunning sights of Dani, he had to close his eyes as he sank down into her. The warmth and pleasant tug of her body was so familiar and yet had been out of reach for so long. It was as if he'd gone without her forever. She wrapped her legs around him, caressing the backs of his thighs with her ankles. He planted both elbows on the bed and combed his fingers into her hair, kissing her unforgettable mouth. She tasted so sweet, even when her tongue did things that made him feel like he'd been a very bad boy.

Dani tilted her hips, allowing him to thrust even deeper. He pressed his lips against her cheek, along her jaw and down her neck. They moved together in that rhythm he knew so well, one that belonged to only them. He hadn't merely missed Dani, he'd missed this closeness with her—where nothing else mattered and the rest of the world could be forgotten. He'd lost his shield when he lost her—or, to be more accurate, when he pushed her away.

Dani's breaths were short and ragged now. The motion of her hips was more insistent, and that only made Cole want to try harder. He pushed up from the bed, holding his torso tight, trying to keep it together while he made his thrusts longer and deeper. His legs were on fire, the pressure coiling in his hips, gathering in his belly. He listened carefully to Dani, watched for clues as she closed her eyes and bit her lower lip, looking so impossibly beautiful and sexy. She turned her head to one side and he kissed her neck, knowing how much she loved that. She arched into him, muscling him closer with her heels.

She didn't have to tell him that she was close. He

could feel the tension inside her. He stayed focused, not ready to give way until she did, even when his mind was fuzzy and the pleasure was knocking at the gates, threatening to barrel through him. He had a hell of a lot to make up for. His performance needed to be spectacular—enough fireworks for a hundred Fourths of July.

Her mouth was slack now, her breaths halting and choppy. She dug her fingers into his shoulders and tightened the grip of her legs. The next thing he knew, she was unraveling, falling apart at the seams in the most stunning way. He watched her, transfixed by the vision, until his climax ran through his body like a freight train headed straight down a mountain. He pressed his hips into her one more time and dropped his head, nestling his face in her neck.

Dani wrapped her arms and legs around him even tighter, humming softly, a habit of hers he'd nearly forgotten about. She hummed after sex. He still had no idea why and she could never explain it, either, beyond the fact that she was happy.

"That was incredible," she muttered into his chest.

Yeah, well, remind me to go without sex for nearly six years. That'll do that to a guy. "It was, Dani. It really was."

He eased to his side and she hopped up from the bed, flitting into the bathroom. How he loved watching her lovely rear end bouncing along in close proximity. He hadn't merely missed Dani. He'd been starved for her. She made him feel more than alive. She made him feel invincible. This high was something he hadn't felt in six years. He hadn't felt this good for even one minute since she left.

That meant he needed to get his priorities straight and figure out what he wanted from her. They couldn't just sleep with each other and walk away—there was too much between them. Too many secrets. But then again, would he ever get her to tell him the truth about her sons? She'd kept things hush-hush for so long.

Dani stopped in the doorway of her bathroom and leaned against it, trailing her finger up and down the jamb. "I almost hate to say this, because I don't want to feed your ego, but you look spectacular in my bed."

"Consider my ego fed. That's the best thing anyone has ever said to me." Laughing, Cole peeled the covers back, offering them in invitation. "Please. Join me in looking spectacular."

Dani climbed into bed and placed a soft and delicate kiss on his lips. Her breasts pressed against his chest, sent the all-hands-on-deck signal straight to his groin. No question this would be his shortest recovery ever. And damn, he wanted another chance at everything they'd just done together. He couldn't wait for more.

Dani slipped her leg between his, rocking her thigh against him. "Ooh. Again?"

He was so hard it nearly made him dizzy. "Yes. And maybe again after that."

Dani didn't hesitate to straddle his hips and take his erection in her hand, guiding him inside her. She sank down onto him, and his eyes drifted shut as her warmth enveloped him. She dropped down and kissed him hard, bouncing her hips in a rhythm that had his head spinning. He curled his fingers into the velvety flesh of her bottom. Tension coiled tightly in his groin and hips. He needed the release again. He thrust more forcefully, lifting her off the bed. She was grinding her hips into his and he could tell from her breaths that he was hitting the right spot. Just when he thought he couldn't take it much longer, Dani called his name and buried her face in his neck. The pleasure rocketed right out of him in waves while Dani let her full bodyweight rest on his, a feeling he'd always loved.

She rolled to his side and curled into him. "So was that a line about not being with any other woman since me?" she asked, still a bit breathless.

Cole pulled her closer, loving the feel of her silky skin against his. "What if it was? Would you be mad?" If only it *was* a line.

"No. I mean, I've fallen for worse, for sure. And you certainly made it worth my while."

"But? I'm sensing a but here."

"But nothing. I'm just surprised. I don't know how often you look in the mirror, but I'm trying to figure out how you stayed out of the beds of every last woman in Royal during that time."

He placed a kiss on her forehead. "Thank you. That's sweet." If he looked back, it seemed impossible, but at the time, he hadn't seen any other way but to stay single. He wasn't about to pull another woman into his orbit. He was damaged goods. Had he looked at women and wanted them? Sure. But his heart hadn't been in it. He didn't see the point. But things were different with Dani, and not just because they had a past. Not because it took no effort at all to want her. She knew the Cole he had been before the glioma was discovered. She knew the old him, the person he wished he could be again.

Trouble was, that was the guy she'd loved, too. And that guy no longer walked the earth.

"I wasn't trying to be sweet. And I already knew there was no other woman when you broke up with me. Megan told me."

He lifted a brow. "How does Megan know the details of my personal life?"

"You've said it yourself a thousand times. This is a small town. People talk."

Cole sucked in a deep breath. Maybe it was time to come clean on this one point. "Yes, I lied about there being someone else. And I'm sorry about that, but I had my reasons."

She shook her head in disbelief. "Just like you had your reasons for waiting until after I left town to quit the Rangers, even when I'd begged you to quit?"

"Would you quit your job if I begged you? That wasn't fair, Dani. I would never ask you to leave behind something you loved."

Dani sat up and cast a look of deep anger at him. "I was trying to guarantee our future together. A long life. I was hoping to grow old with you, Cole. But you threw all of that away."

That stopped him dead. How could he tell her that the thing she'd once hoped for was something he could never give her? Not even now. "Can't we take a break from the past? Just for one day?"

"I don't see how we can, especially when you don't want to talk about it."

From downstairs, the sound of children's voices filtered into the room. Dani slapped the bed and gathered a chunk of the comforter in her hand, narrowly missing Cole's thigh. "The boys are home. You have to get out of here right now." She flew out from under the sheets and began flinging his clothes at him. His shirt hit him square in the face.

"Slow down a minute." He scrambled out from under the covers and started putting on his boxers, hopping on one leg to do it. "I have a good reason for being here."

"Not in my bed, you don't. They're little boys, Cole. They ask lots of questions. You need to put your clothes on right now." Dani was furiously making the bed. Naked. It was the best view ever, but he had zero time to enjoy it.

Dammit.

Cole was turning his shirtsleeves inside out when the boys' voices grew louder. The door was closed, but who knew who long it would be before they burst through it.

Dani raked her dress from the floor and scampered into the bathroom. "Get in here," she whispered to him, loudly.

He followed orders and Dani closed the door behind him. She was still naked, clutching that man-killer dress to her chest. Cole buttoned up his shirt and gave himself a tour. It was like a spa—white marble and sleek fixtures, fluffy white towels, and a shower that might even be bigger than his.

"How many people does this accommodate?" he asked with a leading inflection, pointing to the spacious enclosure wrapped in clear glass.

Dani smacked him on the arm. "There's no time to talk about that. Just finish getting dressed." She pulled a robe from a hook on the wall, and he took his chance to drink in her luscious curves before she wrapped them up in terry cloth and cinched the belt tight.

Cole tucked his dress shirt into his pants, zipped them up and buckled his belt. "Is it okay for me to go out there? I can't spend the whole day in your bathroom. Unless we get to use the shower. For that, I will rearrange my schedule."

"Why are you being so cavalier about all of this?"

He didn't want to tell her the truth—this was a good diversion from the stupid way he'd put his foot in his mouth a few minutes ago. Why he'd walked into the trap of discussing his departure from the Texas Rangers, he had no idea. He made a mental note to avoid the topic at all costs in the future. "It's a little funny, don't you think? Sneaking around and whispering in your bathroom? We're adults."

"And you know absolutely nothing about parenting. It's my job to shield them from stuff like this."

Dani cracked the bathroom door and leaned out. Cole leaned against her, and they both craned their necks.

"Mommy? Is Mr. Sullivan here?"

"We saw his truck outside." About a million tiny knocks accompanied the boys' questions.

Dani closed the bathroom door. "See what you did?"

"What? I gave you a ride home. Last time I checked, that was not a federal offense."

"I have to go answer them. You stay here. I'll let you know when you can come out."

Dani disappeared through the door, shutting it behind her. Cole finished putting his suit back on and neatened his hair, which was wonderfully disheveled after his afternoon delights with Dani. He fetched his shoes from her bedroom floor and was putting them on when Dani returned.

"Okay. The boys are out playing in the backyard with Elena. You can go now." She'd changed into her bathing suit and was wearing a cover-up over it. "I'm going to go join them."

"Maybe I can have them over to swim in my pool again?"

"We'll talk about it."

"Okay, then. I guess I'll go." Cole followed her out of her room and headed downstairs. He hated the cool turn things had taken, but thus was the state of their friendship, or relationship or whatever anyone wanted to call it right now. There were problems lurking in every corner of their past. Dare to poke at one issue and the rest would likely rush out for their hiding place.

"Cole," Dani called from the top of the stairs. He turned and looked up at her, wondering if there was any way they'd ever get their act together. "I'll see you on Tuesday? For the trip to Durango City?"

For once, the investigation had been the absolute last thing on his mind. "Yeah. I'll pick you up at four."

"Perfect."

Cole merely nodded and walked away. *Perfect* was about the last word he would've used to describe the current state of affairs.

Eight

Cole would've been lying if he said that he was feeling completely certain the sting would go off as planned. All of this effort—an entire team of people, a private jet, countless hours and resources, bringing Dani into it—it had to add up to something. If it didn't, there would be no justice for Will or Megan or Jason. Cole couldn't let this operation fail.

"Folks, we'll be landing in a few minutes," the pilot said.

Cole took Dani's hand. "You got everything straight?"

"Yes. You're Chet Pearson, one of the largest private investors in crude oil and natural gas in the US. I'm Melanie Skye, aspiring actress and your girlfriend of six months. I really wish I could've been a chef."

"Too dangerous. We don't want to remind him that he's met you."

"It was a lifetime ago. I mean, I'm memorable, but not that memorable."

Cole managed a nervous grin. "Just stick to the plan, okay? You'll give me a heart attack otherwise."

She slipped her hand from his and picked a tiny piece of lint from her dress. "It's pretty straightforward, isn't it? I do everything I can to ingratiate myself to Sheriff Orson and try to get him to brag to me about how powerful he is and the sneaky things he's done."

"And what else?"

"I don't let you leave my side." She was definitely taking this seriously. She was throwing his exact wording back at him.

"Right. I don't trust that mic they put in your handbag. It's not as reliable as a wire."

"You should've let me pick a dress that would've accommodated one. Then we wouldn't have to worry about that part."

He glanced over at her, memories of the other afternoon threatening to overtake what should've been an entirely professional train of thoughts going through his head. The dress was perfect. Dani was perfect. He loved seeing her in it, and he knew exactly how lucky he was to have had the privilege of taking it off her the other afternoon. It had been such an incredible physical reunion, but could they get on the same page with their other issues? Could he finally just tell her his secret? It had felt good to come out with one untruth the other day, but she hadn't taken it well. There was no telling how she'd react if he finally told her everything.

"You look very handsome in that tux," Dani said.

Cole had gone all out with the Armani, his most expensive pair of cuff links, and his Rolex. No detail was too small for tonight. "Thank you. You look even more amazing now in that dress than you did the other day."

Dani reached out and touched his arm. "Thank you."

Cole stole another eyeful of Dani, but now he was second-guessing the dress. Did it make her too much of a sitting duck? Too enticing? There was no way this sheriff, with a known weakness for beautiful women, didn't glom on to her right away. It was the perfect plan. And that scared the hell out of him.

"Honestly, I'm glad you aren't wearing a wire. I don't want you thinking about being alone with him for even an instant."

"Look. I've been around this guy before. I can handle him. Plus, I won't put myself in danger. The boys need me."

Don't remind me. The plane dipped down, and Cole saw the small airstrip below. "There's still time to back out. You're not obligated to me or this investigation."

She turned and gave him a look of admonishment. "I have to do this for Megan. And for Savannah. I *was* that little girl. The little girl without the family she should have had. I can't let her down. We have to catch the men responsible for Jason's death."

"Okay then, Melanie. It's showtime."

The plane landed safely and taxied down the short runway. After a few moments, the pilot stepped out of the cockpit. "Your car is waiting for you at the bottom of the stairs. He'll bring you right back when you decide to fly home. Enjoy your evening." He winked at Cole but otherwise kept a straight face. The pilot worked for the FBI and would be on hand to leave at a moment's notice if needed.

Cole squeezed Dani's hand three times as a reminder that they were officially in sting mode. From this moment on, they were Chet and Melanie. Eyes could be watching and ears could be listening. Sheriff Orson's influence was all over this damn county. His deputy wouldn't have been so nervous about offering information if that wasn't the case.

As they rode up into the mountains along a winding road, Cole reminded himself that this was for Jason. It was for Savannah and Will and Megan. Rich belonged behind bars for the rest of his life.

Miles away from the landing strip, the car pulled up to an ornately scrolled iron gate. It was flanked by massive stone pillars and tall walls that trailed off into the dense woods on both sides. As the driver buzzed the intercom and requested entry, Cole noticed a security camera panning the length of the car. They drove onto the property, which was sprawling and immaculately landscaped, lit up with dramatic lighting. At the top of the hill—the highest point, as near as Cole could tell—the house sat waiting. It, too, was lit up, glowing in the inky blackness of the night.

"I remember this place," Dani muttered under her breath, referring to the time she'd done a catering job out here years ago. "He made it sound like he was a businessman who just happened to be sheriff."

"No. He's a sheriff involved in business he shouldn't be. That's the reality."

"How are the citizens here not completely up in arms about this place? The man is clearly abusing his power."

"He's greased a lot of palms along the way. Only trouble with that is people will only stay quiet for so long, especially when your misdeeds keep getting worse."

Dani wrapped her arms around herself and nodded. "We need to get this guy good."

They came to a stop, and the driver opened the door on Dani's side. She slid across the seat and climbed out. Cole followed. Now that they were out of the confines of the car, things were about to get that much more real.

"I'll be waiting for you, Mr. Pearson," the driver said to Cole. He, too, was one more agent on-site. That definitely gave Cole a sense of security.

"Thank you. We might be late."

He nodded. "Take as long as you need, sir."

Two armed security guards were waiting outside the front door. "We need to check you for a weapon, sir," one of them said, patting down Cole with little warning. "He's good."

Dani smiled and held up her hands in mock surrender. "I'm sorry, gentlemen, but I can assure you I couldn't hide a gun in this dress if I wanted to."

"Yes, ma'am." The guard seemed embarrassed. "But we need to check your handbag, as well."

With no hesitation, Dani handed it over. "Oh, sure. Just a bunch of tampons in there."

Just as Cole was wondering why in the hell she was choosing to share that bit of information, the guard returned her bag without looking. "I'll take your word for it, ma'am."

Cole grinned and snuggled Dani closer as she hooked her arm in his and they made their way up the stairs to the front door.

A tuxedoed waiter with a silver tray of champagne was waiting inside the door. A young woman with a clipboard was checking names. "You must be Mr. Pearson and Ms. Skye. Sheriff Orson is eager to meet you both."

Dani smiled and said, "We're eager to meet him, too."

As soon as the words came out of her mouth, Cole caught sight of their target, Sheriff Orson. A trim and fit man, he was well groomed, wearing a fitted dark suit and crisp white shirt.

The sheriff noticed them and came right over, introducing himself. "Sheriff Billy Orson. You must be Mr. Pearson and Ms. Skye. Pleased to meet you both." He turned to Cole. "Mr. Pearson, I hope you're going to write me a big fat check this evening. It won't be much fun if you don't."

This guy does not mess around. Cole couldn't believe he'd hardly been through the door before he was the recipient of a thinly veiled threat. "I assure you, I've come here tonight with only the best intentions."

"Glad to hear it." He then turned to Dani. "As for you, Ms. Skye, I hope you will join me for a drink. I'll be sorely disappointed if you say no." The man had the nerve to reach out and take her hand, looping her arm around his and leading her to the far side of the room, where a long line of bar stools sat along a counter with a view of the gourmet kitchen.

It took every ounce of control Cole had in his body not to pounce on the guy. He followed them closely, watching every move. Orson asked Dani to sit at the bar but didn't offer Cole a seat. He did, however, pour them both a drink. He and Dani had agreed ahead of time that they would fake their way through drinking this evening. They needed to be on top of their game.

"Could I get some extra ice?" Dani asked, her voice dripping with sweetness.

"Why of course, you can, beautiful," the sheriff replied. Cole wanted to strangle him.

The sheriff downed his drink in a single gulp and poured himself another, then proceeded to go into his sales pitch to Cole about the pipeline investment. He said everything a wealthy man who wanted to get wealthier could want to hear—that it was not just a gold mine ripe for the taking, but that he was the only person who could get the pipeline approved. He had the contacts with all local authorities. They would do whatever he wanted. He also knew how to put the thumbscrews to what he called "the do-gooder environmental groups." He claimed that he would have no problem rushing through the project and getting the oil flowing, and the money would start rolling in. Sheriff Orson would simply be receiving a generous cut of the deal for his expertise and connections.

Dani hung on every word, and there were a lot of them. The guy would not stop talking. Every time another high-roller guest walked by, the sheriff would pull them into the conversation and start the sales pitch all over again. Cole and Dani endured hours of the sheriff bragging about his power and unfortunately witnessed his inappropriate flirtation and not-so-subtle innuendo with the women at the party. By the end of it, Cole felt like he needed to take a shower.

The sheriff was very good at closing the deal, though. He got signed investment agreements from every guest at the party.

"Are you ready to sign on the dotted line, Mr. Pearson?" Orson asked now that Cole was the sole remaining holdout.

"What do you think, Melanie?" Cole asked Dani the question as if it actually mattered. Chet Pearson's signature meant nothing.

"I think you should do it. Then we can have a drink to celebrate."

The sheriff squared his sights on Dani. "I'm not

sure which is better, hearing those words or hearing them come out of your gorgeous mouth."

Cole glanced at her as she smiled through what had to be unimaginable disgust. All he could think was that they had to steer this conversation in the right direction, or Sheriff Orson was going to be dead. A few more comments like that about Dani, and Cole would have to kill him with his bare hands.

The other guests had departed, meaning Dani's determination to nail Sheriff Orson to the wall was as strong as ever. After hours of watching him be inappropriate with women and boastful with men, he'd proven himself to be exactly what Dani had thought the first time she'd met him—scum of the highest order. Knowing that he'd played the pivotal role in the cover-up of Jason's death made it that much more certain. Now they just needed to get him to talk.

"Sheriff, now that Mr. Pearson has signed your agreement and we've had our celebratory drink, I think we should go. I'm afraid we've overstayed our welcome." She had no intention of leaving. She just wanted to threaten him with it.

"Little lady, as long as you're wearing that dress, you can stay as long as you like." Sheriff Orson was slurring his words now. All the drinks he'd had were taking effect. Little did the sheriff know that Cole and Dani had been dumping their drinks into a nearby potted plant all night.

Dani really hated being called *little lady*. "Sheriff, I have to say that you have quite an impressive

home. I don't know that I've ever seen a public servant with such a grand setup."

Cole took a sip of his drink but stayed otherwise
quiet, letting her take the reins.

"Public servant? Is that what you think of me?
The people of this county are damn lucky to have
me. I work hard."

Judging by the way he was raising his voice, Dani
knew this was the right approach. Men like Sheriff
Orson felt that they weren't like everyone else. They
were above the law and the rules simply didn't apply
to them. "I'm not saying you don't work hard. I'm
sure you do. I just wasn't aware that driving around
in a car with a shotgun all day was so lucrative."

"I have business interests on the side. A man is
entitled to augment his salary."

"Of course. Like your little pipeline, which sounds
like such a neat project." Dani was sure to lend extra
emphasis to *little* and *neat*. She knew how much ego-
tistical men hated to be dismissed like that.

"It's not a little pipeline. It's a massive project.
We're talking millions of dollars on the line."

"Million with an *M*, right? Not billions, like they
would have in Alaska or the Dakotas."

"Excuse me?" The sheriff's eyes blazed with an
anger that made Dani distinctly uncomfortable. She
had to calm him down a bit.

She reached out and touched his arm. "I'm not
trying to disparage your hard work. I'm guessing
you're by far the most powerful man in this corner
of the world."

His shoulders visibly relaxed, and Dani felt as though she could breathe again.

"Oh, absolutely," Cole chimed in.

The sheriff glanced over at him, and Dani had the distinct impression that she wasn't going to get anywhere with Cole in the room. His role as protector was getting in the way.

"If you'll excuse me, I need to visit the little cowboys' room," the sheriff said.

Dani smiled, thinking that only a complete buffoon of a grown man would refer to it as that. As soon as he was out of sight, she grabbed Cole's arm.

"You have to leave me alone with him. Just for a few minutes. I think I can get him to say it."

Cole shook his head. "No way, Dani. It's too dangerous." His jaw was firmly set and he stood a little straighter. He was determined to keep her safe. It was so damn sexy, even if it was giving her problems.

"My purse is sitting right there. Just go to the bathroom when he's done and listen. If I'm not getting anywhere after five minutes, come back and we'll try something new."

He grasped her bare shoulder with his warm hand, his thumb landing on her clavicle, sending a zip of electricity through her. "I don't like this."

From the hall, she heard the sound of a toilet flushing and water running. "I can do it. Just give me a chance."

"Can I pour y'all another drink?" Sheriff Orson asked, returning to the room, his presence making Dani's skin crawl.

"Oh, sure," Dani answered. "How about you, Chet? Another drink?" She stared him down as subtly as she could.

Cole swallowed hard enough that she could see his Adam's apple bob up and down. "That sounds great. But I think I need to use the washroom, as well. I'll be back in a few."

Bingo.

As soon as Cole disappeared down the hall, the sheriff made his move, as she'd been certain he would. "What's the deal with you and Chet there? He doesn't really seem like your type."

"You've only known me for a few hours. How did you deduce that?"

"Gorgeous woman like you deserves a man with money and power. Chet seems to have the first, but that's about it."

She took a calm breath, even though her stomach was churning. "I appreciate the gesture, Sheriff, but I'm not sure you wield the kind of power that really turns a woman on." She bit her lower lip, looking into his eyes and seeing nothing but pure evil. In her head, she repeated the reasons she was here. *Do this for Megan. Do it for Savannah.*

"I have more power than you could imagine." He leaned against the kitchen counter, narrowing his sights on her cleavage.

Dani had no choice but to sit a little straighter and employ her assets. "Somehow I doubt that."

"Oh, yeah?"

She nodded confidently, feeling nothing of the sort on the inside. "Sorry, but yeah."

He moved in on her, coming closer until he was only inches away. With him standing and her sitting on the bar stool, she felt overpowered. Overmatched. "I can make a person disappear."

Dani laughed, but it was out of sheer nervousness. *Oh my God. He's going to say it.* "Like a magician? Or for real?"

"For real. I've done it many times. Did it to a man just a few weeks ago."

She dared to look up at his face, stretching her neck and making herself more vulnerable to him, knowing she only had a few more seconds until Cole would be back. "You were daring enough to do that? Aren't you afraid of getting caught?"

Sheriff Orson shrugged it off. "I told you, darling. I'm in charge here. A man showed up and told me he needed a body cremated, ASAP. I took his money, put a phony name on the coroner's report and told them to flick the switch."

Before Dani knew what was happening, the front door burst open and a stream of men wearing navy jackets emblazoned with FBI stormed inside. They were all over Sheriff Orson, bringing his hands behind his back, reading him his rights and slapping handcuffs on him.

The sheriff stared her down. "You bitch."

Dani didn't know what else to do other than smile. She watched as he was led away, overcome with the most intense rush of relief and accomplishment she'd felt in her entire life. Well, aside from when the twins had been born. That was no small feat, either.

She was still standing there in a daze when she felt Cole's presence and he wrapped his arm around her shoulder. "You were unbelievable. I'm so impressed."

She turned to him and looked up into his gorgeous blue eyes, feeling almost as if she was living outside her body. Everything was surreal right now. "You are?"

"Are you kidding? I heard every word. I never went to the bathroom. I was standing right around the corner, ready to pounce. I couldn't have done this without you. I hope you know that."

It meant so much to hear him say that. Having Cole's approval and appreciation felt so good. Six years ago, she'd lived for it. Now that she had a taste of it again, it brought back a flood of the best feelings between them. They'd been as rock solid as a couple could be. Could they have that again? "I couldn't have done it without *you*. You believed in me. You believed I could do it. And you let me run with it, even when things were getting a little hairy."

Cole laughed. "You definitely waded into some waters I wasn't quite sure of."

"And you trusted me." She didn't take having Cole's trust lightly. That made her extra appreciative of it now, and that much more scared of losing it. Would he forgive her when she told him about the boys? She knew now that no matter what Cole's secret was, even if he never told her, she had to tell him about the boys. And if that killed the trust, she'd just have to rebuild it, brick by brick.

"Of course I did, Dani. I never doubted you could pull this off. I was just waiting to see how you were going to do it."

Just then a tall redheaded woman with a pretty sizable baby bump strolled over, wearing the same jacket the other agents were. She held out her hand for Dani. "Special Agent Marjorie Stanton. I've conducted an awful lot of sting operations in my day, and I have to tell you that was a top-notch performance."

"You were listening, too?"

"Down the street in a van. I heard every word. If you ever decide to give up your culinary career, give me a call." A walkie-talkie at her hip buzzed. "I'm sorry. I need to grab this. Cole, I'll talk to you tomorrow when we're all back in Royal. Bird is closing in on Richard Lowell's stash. We're getting close to catching him and putting him away."

"Great news. I'll get the update tomorrow." Cole took Dani's hand. "I know this is an awful lot of excitement, but are you ready to get out of here?"

"Are you kidding? I never want to come back. What a slimeball."

"A slimeball who's about to go away for a very long time. Right after he gives up Richard Lowell."

"Music to my ears. Now let's get back to the plane." All Dani wanted right now, was for the world to go away so she could be alone with Cole.

Nine

As soon as the plane was up in the air, Cole felt true relief. They'd accomplished what they came to do. He and the team were a monumental step closer to putting Rich away. He'd been working so hard for a major breakthrough like this, that he hadn't had the chance to consider how incredible it would feel to be closer to this goal. And he couldn't have done it without Dani.

He looked over at her, still so stunning in that dress, except now she was even more desirable. They were a team tonight and a damn good one. There was just something about their connection that brought out the best in each of them. Could they be a team again? He'd been asking himself that question non-stop since they'd made love at her house. She made him feel so alive. She made him a better version of himself. He couldn't imagine going back to the way he'd been for the last six years. That version of Cole Sullivan was sleepwalking through life. He couldn't do that to himself anymore.

"Can I just tell you that the way you handled yourself tonight was so damn sexy?" he asked.

She blushed and smiled. "You know what was really sexy? Having you there to protect me." She reached down and took his hand in hers, rubbing her thumb along his knuckles. "It made me do and say things I never thought I could."

The darkened airplane cabin was romantic and even felt private, with the captain up in the cockpit and he and Dani alone in the last row. All Cole could think about was kissing her supple mouth. He moved in, and just like a wish granted, Dani raised her lips to him. They fell into a kiss that was immediately passionate. Maybe it was the thrill of what they'd just been through, but it was clear they were both turned on. Dani dug her fingers into his scalp, and her tongue teased his. Cole tried to get his arms around her, but the stupid armrest was in the way.

"Come here," he said.

Dani looked at him, her lips full, her mouth slack with surprise. "Come here?"

"Yes. Come and get in my lap. I need you in my arms. I need to kiss you for real."

A mischievous smile tugged at her lips. "Are you serious?"

Cole groaned. "I have never been more serious in my entire life. Get over here."

"Okay." Dani unlatched her seat belt and stood, then sat across his lap and put her arm around his neck.

"I thought I'd died and gone to heaven the other day when I got to take this dress off you," Cole muttered against the soft skin of her neck. "I just want to do it again."

"I don't think you can really take it all the way off me this time," Dani countered. "If the pilot looks back here, I'd like at least a slight chance of saving my pride."

Cole unzipped her dress and dragged the straps down her arms. Her breasts were bare to him, her nipples standing at attention in the cool air of the plane. He lowered his lips and drew one into his mouth. Dani responded by moving her bottom in circles against his crotch. She was so sexy it boggled the mind, but knowing that they could get caught added a whole new level of sexiness to this.

Dani dug her fingers into his hair and kissed him deeply, rotating her hips in maddening circles. He planted a hand on her ass and pulled her even closer, wanting no distance between them. The heat was building fast, but they were still wearing too many clothes. "I need to be inside you, Dani."

She reared back her head, and her eyes popped wide. "What if we get caught?"

"Then we get caught. No jury in the world would convict me if they saw you in this dress."

"You're a bad boy, Cole Sullivan." She eased off his lap, hunching down behind the seats, and reached under her dress, shimmying her panties past her hips and leaving them on the floor.

"Plus, I probably won't last very long."

"You're not exactly selling it." She cocked an eyebrow at him.

"Don't worry. I'll be sure you reach your final destination." Cole had unbuttoned his pants and tugged them and his boxer briefs past his hips. Perched on the edge of his seat, he reclined back.

Dani lifted her dress to the middle of her thighs and, one at a time, bracketed his hips with her knees. Her breasts were bare to him, her nipples tight and hard, her hair slightly mussed. He wasn't sure he'd ever seen a hotter sight in all his life.

He took himself in hand and slipped inside Dani's body. He grappled with the incredible sensation as she sank down onto him, her slick heat molding around him, holding on to him tight. It felt unimaginably good, just as it had the other day. Dammit, he and Dani were just right. Everything today had proven that. It made him want to work that much harder for what had once seemed completely out of reach—a future. With her.

Dani rotated her hips in near-perfect figure-eights. It was enough to make Cole rocket into space, but he had to do better than a teenaged boy. Dani changed her motion, rocking forward and back against him. "I need to see your chest," she murmured, unbuttoning his shirt. She spread her hands across his skin and then kissed him as the pleasure began coiling tightly in his belly.

"Well, folks, looks like we've got a bit of turbulence ahead," the captain said over the PA.

Dani and Cole both froze. Her chest was heaving, she was breathing so hard.

"Just hold on tight back there and I'll get you out of this as soon as I can," the captain said.

Dani giggled, then went back to kissing him, back to moving her hips in those mind-bending rotations. The plane dropped a few feet and they both sucked in a breath, but neither broke the kiss. Right now, even gravity was not a concern.

Dani's breaths were getting choppy, but Cole could tell she wasn't quite getting what she wanted. She was fitful in his arms, now kissing his neck and burying her forehead into the seat back behind him. He shifted one of his hands under her dress and, using his thumb, found her center. His other hand was at the small of her back, pushing her against his hand.

"Yes," Dani gasped. "Right there."

The plane bounced and pitched. Cole blocked it out. He had Dani in his arms, and that was all that mattered right now. He hadn't felt so aligned with her in a long time, between their amazing teamwork at the party tonight and now, handing their fate over to gravity and turbulence and Mother Nature. As ecstasy flamed in his belly and Dani muttered in his ear for more, he was hit again by the realization this was the way things should be. As crazy and dangerous as ever, he and Dani should always be like this. Together.

Dani muffled her voice in Cole's shoulder when she reached her peak, and he pulled her tight against his chest as the pleasure charged through him.

She settled her head against his chest. "Tonight meant a lot to me, Cole. That you were proud of me."

That struck him as a bit amazing. Most of the time, Dani seemed like she didn't need anyone's approval. "It did?"

She slowly raised her head and nodded. Her eyes were misty.

"You okay, Dani?" He reached up and cupped her cheek.

She turned into his touch immediately, pressing her lips to the inside of his hand. "I am. I just didn't want to let it go unsaid."

He pulled her close again, kissing the top of her head while her words cycled through his head. Leaving things gone unsaid had torn them apart. He simply hadn't been able to utter the words. He hadn't had the courage to say that he was a man with a ticking time bomb in his head. That was only one big secret between them now, though. Cameron and Colin had to be his. His gut was telling him they were. All of this needed to come to light. All of it. And with the sting behind them, that was the most pressing issue he and Dani faced. Once that dirty laundry was aired, would they still be okay? And what did "okay" even entail? His glioma was never going away. That much would never, ever change.

A still quiet Dani carefully climbed off Cole's lap and sat down in her seat, replacing the straps of her dress and turning so Cole could help her zip up the back. She smoothed her hair while peering over the tops of the seats in front of them.

"You don't think he heard us, do you?"

Cole shrugged. "Not much we can do about it now." He'd gotten his pants sorted out by that point. Now to finish buttoning his shirt.

Dani leaned across the armrest and gave him a kiss. "Never a dull moment with you, is there?"

"You know me. Total adrenaline junkie."

"I'd better sneak into the bathroom and tidy up. God only knows how bad my makeup looks right now." She bent down and plucked her panties from the floor. "Yikes. Can't forget these." She scooted past him.

Cole's mind started making plans as soon as Dani was gone. Would she be up for coming out to the ranch with him tonight? Or would she invite him over to her house? He couldn't stand the thought of putting off his admission or his questions about the boys any longer. It had to happen tonight. He decided he would ask her as soon as they were back in his truck and leaving the airfield.

Dani returned and Cole took his chance to use the restroom and put his clothes back together in a way that made it look at least slightly less obvious that he and Dani had just had sex on the plane. As he strolled back down the aisle, he was struck by a sharp pain at his temple. He grabbed the seat back and clamped his eyes shut. He couldn't see past the pain. It was like a thunderbolt of white, like someone was shining a searchlight square in his eyes.

"Cole. Are you okay?" Dani asked.

His eyes were still shut. The instant he tried to open them, he regretted it. The flash of agony that ripped through his head was unlike anything he'd ever experienced. And he'd been through a lot of pain in his life. The plane was dipping and pitching again. He found it hard to stand up straight. Somewhere he could hear Dani's voice, but it was coming in and out, like someone was turning the dial on a radio.

He could feel her touch, though, her insistent hands on his biceps pulling him down. The next thing he knew he was sitting.

"Cole Sullivan, talk to me right now or I will never speak to you again."

There was her voice. He heard it clear as a whistle now. It made him smile, but only slightly. Just moving his lips made his head hurt more.

"Headache," he managed to say. "Bad headache."

"Like a migraine?"

Cole nodded. He'd never had a migraine before, but his mother suffered from them and he knew that they often involved extreme reactions to light and they could came on very suddenly. He hoped to hell a migraine was all it was.

"What can I do?"

He shook his head as slightly as possible. What could she do? Nothing right now. "Hold my hand."

She wrapped her fingers around his. That prompted

another smile from him, one that hurt less than the last one. Maybe this wasn't a big deal. He really hoped that was the case.

"Cole, you're worrying me."

"I'll be fine." His words were raspy and dry. He almost didn't recognize his own voice.

"We're supposed to land in ten minutes. We can take you straight to the hospital."

Cole shook his head. He didn't even care how much it hurt. He did not want to go there. Bad things happened there. Bad news. Life-altering news. He couldn't live with that. Not when he had a chance to have Dani again.

Aside from the time the boys got strep throat, Dani had never been so worried in her whole life. She held on to Cole's hand, studying every movement of his face since he wasn't saying much. His eyes were closed, but the muscles of his forehead and around his eyes twitched from time to time. He was in immense pain. She could see the way he flinched from nothing at all.

"Folks, we're making our final approach into Royal," the captain said.

As the nose of the plane dipped down, Dani wrapped her other hand around Cole's, not wanting to let go. Worry was consuming her. Cole was tough as nails. Almost too tough. He did not like for people to see him in a compromised state—he saw it as weakness. Dani only saw how human he was. Which meant whatever was going on right now was bad. How could she go from the high of the sting to the slow burn of making love on the plane to being worried sick about Cole? It was a miracle she could manage a single coherent thought right now.

Luckily, the landing was smooth as silk. Dani didn't want anything jostling Cole too much. "You stay right here. I'll go get the car and bring it around. Then I'll get the pilot to help me get you off this plane."

Cole shook his head and opened one eye. "I'm fine."

"You are not fine. Keep your butt in this seat and I'll be right back."

As if Dani needed confirmation that Cole was indeed hurting badly, he nodded and slumped back in the chair. He almost never listened to her. Again, the worry ate at her. What in the world was going on?

She got the pilot up to speed and he sat with Cole while Dani ran—in heels and her mermaid dress, no less—to get Cole's car. Thank goodness they'd been able to fly in a private plane in and out of Royal. She never would've been able to get him through the airport terminal in Houston. She would've needed a wheelchair, and if she knew one thing about Cole, it was that he would not put up with that. The amount of negotiating she and the head nurse at Royal Memorial had had to do after his big accident six years ago was ridiculous. Cole was as stubborn as a mule.

She tore up the stairs to the plane. Cole was in the same spot, but his eyes were open and he was talking to the pilot. Dani had to wonder if he was actually feeling better or if he was just putting on a show because there was another man present.

"How are we doing?" she asked.

"Better," Cole replied, getting out of his seat a bit more easily than he'd been moving before she'd gone to get the car.

"Well, good. Thank you," she said to the pilot. "I really appreciate your help."

"No problem."

Dani took Cole's hand and they walked off the plane, Dani going first down the stairs. She got him into the passenger seat, but he was already grumbling. He really was the worst patient.

"You know, most people say they have a headache before sex, not after," she said when she got into the driver's seat.

Cole clicked his seat belt. "Very funny. You know I would never turn down sex. Not even right now."

Dani started his truck and put it into gear. "Somehow I doubt that." She pulled past the security gate. "I know the hospital isn't your favorite place, and I know you already said you don't want to go, but I really think I should take you."

"I really don't want to go tonight. I'm sure it's nothing. Probably just the stress of the sting. I can go see the doctor in the morning if I'm still in pain."

"Well, I don't feel comfortable with the idea of you being alone tonight. And I'd rather not stay out at the ranch. I don't like being away when the boys get up in the morning, and we'll be closer to the hospital at my house."

"Are you inviting me to sleep over?"

"Yes. But there will be no sex. Just resting. And if you aren't feeling completely better in the morning, I'm taking you to the doctor."

"But—"

Dani held up a finger. "No buts. My rules."

"Yes, ma'am."

"And who's your doctor? I need to know who to call."

"Dr. Lee. Royal Memorial," he muttered.

"Good."

The drive to her place was thankfully short, especially this late. It was nearly 2:00 a.m. by the time they got to the house. Between the adrenaline rush of the sting and sex on an airplane, Dani was exhausted, but she managed to help Cole upstairs to her room.

"We need to get you out of that suit," she said.

He grinned, but she could see a wince around his eyes. He was still in a lot of pain.

"Get your mind out of the gutter. You're going straight to bed. To sleep."

With some rambling commentary from him about how she was being a stick in the mud, Dani was able to help him take his pants and shirt off and got him into bed.

She sat on the edge of the mattress right next to him. It was impossible to not think about the last time she'd taken care of Cole, in the weeks after the accident. She'd always worried so much about his job, and then the near worst had happened. At least she hadn't lost him, she'd told herself over and over again. That would've been an unbearable loss. He was her everything then—her sun and moon, the reason for getting out of bed in the morning. Her career was important to her and she loved to cook, but that didn't take up space in her heart the way Cole did.

When someone you cared about that much had a brush with death, it made you realize exactly how much you loved them. Honestly, it scared her at first, walking into that hospital and understanding exactly how much was on the line. It was overwhelming—creating a burning pit in her belly, making her feel cold and helpless at the same time.

One of the worst parts was the scene that unfolded in the waiting room while he underwent surgery. Cole's family had been there, and his mother got downright territorial about it, trying to send Dani home. "We only need family here right now," she'd said. Dani would've been hurt if she wasn't so damn mad about that. His parents had never approved of her, the kid from the wrong side of the tracks, no impressive family lineage to back her up. "We can call you when he wakes up," she'd said. Dani's only response to that had been to grit her teeth and politely reply, "I love your son, Mrs. Sullivan. So, no, I will not be going home."

Dani had loved Cole deeply before that day, but it was a young love built on invincibility. She'd worried about his job, but the reality of her worst nightmare was almost more than she could bear. She threw herself into his recovery, doting on him, making sure he had everything he needed. And, impossibly, her love for him only grew. It reached depths she had never imagined. It was impossible during those moments not to think about the what-ifs. *What if he'd been paralyzed? What if he'd been burned?* Or even worse, *What if he hadn't made it out alive?* Thoughts like that made her cry her eyes out when she was alone. She was so thankful. He was so lucky. They were incredibly fortunate to have each other and to have found each other. She had to hold on to Cole's love forever. She'd never, ever known a love like the one she had with Cole at that time. Not even close.

Which made the breakup not only more crushing, it had made it impossible to believe. Of course you wouldn't break up with the person who had just nursed you back to health and shown you unconditional love in the face of dire circumstances, ones you were facing because you had refused to do the one thing your loved one had begged you to do—quit your job. Who would do that? Who would take that kind of love and devotion and throw it away?

Cole Sullivan, that was who. And she was still desperate for the answer to one question—why?

He settled back in bed and closed his eyes. "Thank you," he said. "I think I just need to get some sleep. I'm sure I'll be feeling much better in the morning."

Dani snugged the covers up around his shoulders, even when it denied her one of her favorite views—his glorious chest. "I'm sure you will be, too." She then did the one thing she probably shouldn't have—

she leaned forward and placed a single, tender kiss on his temple. Tears misted her eyes the instant she did it. She couldn't deny what was in her heart now. She loved Cole just as much as she'd ever loved him. Possibly more. She'd spent every day of the last six years caring for the most beautiful extension of him—his two sons. It was a perpetual reminder of how much good there was in him, despite the things he'd done to hurt her.

But that realization also sent the guilt crushing down. If Cole had done the unimaginable when he'd ended their relationship, Dani had done something far worse. She'd kept his own children from him. She'd had every good reason in the world when they were thousands of miles away from each other, but now that they were in the same place again, she couldn't help but feel sick about it. Even when she'd given him a second chance and sent him that letter right before the boys were born. No, he hadn't replied, but she also hadn't told him what was *really* going on.

Cole's breaths grew more even, and Dani got up to change her clothes and wash her face. Looking into the bathroom mirror, she had to wonder what was going to become of her. Was Cole just enjoying their undeniable physical attraction? Or was he serious about her? Did he want a second chance? She didn't want to admit to herself just how badly she wanted it. Right now, it felt like she might not be able to live through it if the answer was no. But she'd told herself that she would never again put that much stock in Cole, and here she was, pinning a bunch of hope on what he wanted. What about what she wanted? Didn't that count just as much?

What do you want? Dani could hear the question crystal clear in her head, but the answer wasn't quite so quick to come. It was complicated. The minute she'd become a mother, the boys became an inextricable part of this equation. What they wanted and needed was equally important, possibly more so. She wanted stability for them. She wanted a good life where they could count on everything and everyone around them. She wanted green grass, clean air and laughter in the backyard, giggles at the dinner table, and bedtime stories that went on too long. *Just one more, Mommy.* And after the boys gave in to sleep each night, she wanted someone to talk it all over with. She wanted a partner, someone to share all this good she'd managed to build. She wanted everything she'd thought was possible before Cole ended it with her.

She flipped off the bathroom light and leaned against the door frame, watching Cole sleep in the soft glow of the lamp on her side of the bed. What in the world had happened on that day nearly six years ago? What had gone through that head of his that made him want to throw away what they had? Her gut was telling her that he'd left out some key piece of information. He was hiding something from her. If they had any chance of moving forward, he was going to have to come clean. Yes, she had her own secrets to confess, but he'd set them on this path. And there was no going back.

She walked around to the far side of the room and turned off the light, climbing into bed. She didn't want to disturb his sleep, but she wanted to be close to him. She couldn't help it. She scooted closer, wrapping her hand around his arm and stretching out beside him. Closing her eyes, she drew in his smell—warm cedar and soap. She knew she had to get some sleep. She and Cole had a lot to talk about in the morning. She couldn't endure another day of not knowing what he wanted from her. And that was going to involve her own confession, one that had been waiting too long.

Ten

Cole hadn't slept. He'd only slipped in and out of consciousness. During the moments when he came to, the pain reminded him to keep his eyes closed and his body still and to try to claim real slumber. It was his only escape from the agony and the worry.

And now that the Texas sun was peeking through his eyelids, he was going to have to face reality. His headache had not improved—it had only settled in. The doctors had warned him, told him to watch out for events like this. They'd told him he needed to come in right away when it happened. He'd already ignored those orders by coming to Dani's last night. But the truth was that he was scared. He'd seen a glimmer of what his future could hold and just like that, his body was trying to take it away. There was some part of him that had hoped the headache would simply go away. Unfortunately, it hadn't. He couldn't ignore what he needed to do anymore.

"Morning." Dani's sweet voice was a brief respite from the chaos in his head. "How are you doing?"

He still hadn't fully committed to opening his eyes, so he rolled to his side to put the window behind him. Light was not his friend right now. He went slowly, and he couldn't have had a lovelier vision to wake up to—Dani with her hair up in a high ponytail, wearing light pink pajamas and offering him a cup of coffee. Still, it took more effort to keep his eyes open than could ever be considered normal.

"I gotta be honest. I'm feeling pretty rough."

She caressed his arm. "Headache's no better?"

"No."

"Okay. Well, I looked up the number for Dr. Lee's office and called them. They said they want to see you as soon as we can get there."

Panic coursed through Cole's body. What if the doctor's office slipped and told her about his condition? "You called Dr. Lee? What did he say?"

"I only spoke to the nurse. She just said you should come in. That was all. He's doing rounds at the hospital this morning and will see you as soon as we get there."

He sighed and resigned himself to the fact that even though it was the last thing he wanted to do today, he was going to have to see the doctor. "I guess I should get dressed."

"You want to wear a suit to the doctor's office? I

could call one of your brothers and ask them to bring you some different clothes."

"I have a pair of jeans and a T-shirt in a duffel in the truck."

"Oh, right. A rancher never knows when he's going to get dirty."

He forced a smile. "Exactly."

"I'll get it. You stay put."

Dani was back a few minutes later with his things, and Cole did his best to soldier through the most mundane of tasks—going to the bathroom, putting on clean clothes.

"Is it okay if we take my car? I'll leave the mini-van for Elena and the boys." she asked. "No offense, but I hate driving your truck."

As if he was in any position to argue with her. "Yeah. No problem." He tried to look on the bright side. With his car there, he'd have an excuse to come back to Dani's house as soon as the doctor gave him some real painkillers and sent him on his way. Then they could have their talk.

Dani took charge when they arrived at Royal Memorial, getting them right into a triage room. The nurse took his vitals and got him settled on the exam table, but the minute they were left waiting, the bad memories started to come back, and that made his head pound even worse. The fluorescent lights overhead were nightmarishly bright, and that hospital smell was everywhere. Cole couldn't escape it.

"You doing okay?" Dani asked.

It took a ridiculous amount of effort to nod. "Yep."

He hadn't realized until then that she was holding his hand. Had it become that comfortable? Or was he that out of tune with what was going on around him right now? Too stuck in his own body? That had been a huge symptom of the last six years—feeling trapped. How else was a man to feel when he was saddled with a condition from which he could never escape?

The telltale sound of the exam room curtain sliding on its rails came. "I spoke to Dr. Lee," a voice said. "He wants to go ahead and do an MRI first, and then he'll see you after that."

Cole broke out into a cold sweat. "I just need some painkillers." He didn't want to know if this was all because the tumor had grown. He didn't want to know if this was the beginning of the end. Plus, he hadn't had a chance to talk to Dani yet and he couldn't see straight right now, let alone think straight.

"Isn't that a little excessive?" Dani asked. "He just has a migraine."

"Given his history, Dr. Lee felt it was not only the most logical step, it was the only course of action right now."

"His history?" Dani's voice was nothing if not incredulous. She was mystified by what was going on. If only she knew. "What history? His accident? Is there something I don't know?"

"I'm sorry, but are you family?" The nurse had taken a tone that he knew Dani would hate.

Cole's mind raced. He would have done anything to put this conversation on pause, but his thoughts weren't merely jumbled, they were fighting each other. He wanted Dani there, but he wanted to be able to break this news to her the right way. Not in the hospital. Not when he was in so much pain. "She's my girlfriend." The words just came out. They were the only thing that made sense. Cole forced his eyes open, only to see a truly surprised Dani standing next to him.

"I'm sorry, but I can only discuss the patient's history with a spouse or next of kin. Mr. Sullivan, I'm going to check in with the radiologist to find out how long before we can get you in."

As soon as the nurse left, Dani whipped around and looked Cole square in the eye. "What does she mean when she says your history?"

Cole dug as deep as he ever had for strength. He needed the presence of mind to say this clearly. He needed the stamina to fight through the pain and look Dani in the eye. He needed the courage to tell her the most difficult and damning detail of his life.

"When the doctors did the MRI the day after my accident, they discovered a glioma. It's a small tumor in a part of my brain they can't reach. It's inoperable. It's not going away. It might get bigger. It could very well be the thing that kills me."

"Oh my God." Dani clamped her hand over her mouth. Her eyes were hurt. She was starting to cry. Was she devastated to hear the news? Or was it because he'd kept it from her all this time?

"That's my secret, Dani. I never told you because I wanted you to live a long life with someone who could be there for the whole thing." Cole could hear his own voice starting to fall apart.

"Cole. No," Dani said.

The nurse returned, and Cole could see the gurney coming for him. "Mr. Sullivan, we need to get you in right now. Dr. Lee wants these results as soon as possible."

The nurse helped him up from the exam table and onto the gurney. He could hardly look at Dani, fearing her reaction. She'd said so little. Too little. He felt even more nauseous now than he had when he'd first gotten this headache. Or the day he'd gotten the worst news.

The orderly began pushing Cole out of the room.

"No. Wait. Stop," Dani said. Her voice was nothing but desperation. Cole had no idea if it was because she was worried or if it was because she was trying to understand his betrayal.

The nurse grasped both of her arms. "Ma'am. You need to stay here. He needs to go in for that test right away."

The orderly kept going, down the hall, away from Dani. It was such a metaphor for everything that had happened between them, and the way things had gone so haywire. Just when he was ready to tell her his secret, the headache stopped him in his tracks. Just when he was ready to ask her if they had a future together, this thing in his head was stepping in and saying, *Not so fast, buddy.*

They wheeled Cole into the MRI room, where the hum of the machine was deafening and everything around him was cold and white and sterile. This was the room where he got the worst news of his life. This where he'd started to lose everything.

Was that going to happen all over again? Would Dani ever forgive him for the things he hadn't said? Or was this MRI about to tell him that none of it mattered, anyway?

Dani stood in Cole's room, frozen.

A tumor. *Cole has a tumor.* She couldn't believe this was happening. Just when she'd learned to trust him again, the truth threw her for far more than a loop. She couldn't even be mad at him right now. All she could do was worry. What were the doctors going to say? And would she and Cole ever be able to move beyond whatever that news was?

Dani's phone rang and it rattled her back to the here-and-now. She dug in her bag, fumbling past her wallet, keys, lipstick, and a million other things. When she finally found her phone, Elena's name was on the caller ID.

"Hello," Dani said.

"Oh, thank God you answered. I'm super sick, Dani. It just hit me like a ton of bricks."

Dani's first instinct was to start walking to her car. She could not believe this day. She didn't think it was possible for her to worry any more than she already was. "What's wrong?"

"I think I've come down with a stomach virus or maybe food poisoning. I can't keep any food down. Or anything at all, actually. I can't watch the boys the way they need to be watched. I'm running to the bathroom every ten minutes. And I don't want them to catch this if it's contagious."

"I'm on my way. I'll get there as fast as I can. Can I pick you anything up on my way home?"

"No, thank you. I just need a break."

Dani ended her call with Elena and quickly scrolled through her contacts for Cole's brother Sam's number. As soon as she had the number ringing on speakerphone, Dani climbed into her car, jammed the ignition button and sped out of the parking lot.

"Dani Moore," Sam answered. "This is a surprise."

"Hey Sam. Do you have a second to talk?"

"For you? Always." Sam was such a charmer.

"I'm calling to let you know that Cole's in the hospital because of a bad headache. They're doing an MRI right now, but I had to leave to tend to something at home. Can you go and make sure he's not alone? I don't want him coming back to an empty room if he doesn't have to."

"Is he okay? Did something happen after the sting?"

"He got a blistering headache pretty soon after. I tried to get him to see a doctor last night, but he wanted to try and sleep it off. That didn't work."

"Sounds like Cole. You know how he feels about doctors."

Dani choked back a sigh. "So do you know about his condition?" Dani wasn't sure who knew what anymore. Thus was the problem with secrets. All the more reason to come out with hers, if she got the chance.

"Did he tell you?"

Dani felt like she and Sam were talking in code, tiptoeing around the truth. "If you're talking about what they discovered in that MRI six years ago, yes."

Sam blew out a breath. "I'm glad to hear he told you."

"Me, too. I just wish I'd had the chance to talk to him about it before they wheeled him down the hall. I'm sick with worry. Someone should be there."

"Don't worry. I'll get over there right now."

"Will you let him know that I'm thinking about him? And let him know I'm ready to talk whenever he wants to. His truck is at my house, but we can sort that out later. It's not a problem for it to stay here as long as possible."

"Thank you for being there for my brother, Dani. You've always been a rock for him."

"Maybe on the outside. On the inside, I'm tied up in knots." Dani turned into her neighborhood and pulled past the security gate.

"That's what you get with my brother." Sam cleared his throat. "I know this is none of my business, and you can tell me to take a hike, but are you two back together?"

Dani shook her head when she caught sight of Cole's truck in her driveway. It was not only a visual of what could be, it was a reminder of everything that was wrong. What was he going through right now? What was happening? Was he okay? "I don't know yet. We've got some things we need to work out." That felt like the understatement of the century, but at least she knew a little bit of what was behind their breakup. "Hey, Sam. I just got home, so I need to run."

"Oh, yeah. Sure. I need to get my butt to the hospital. Thanks so much for keeping me in the loop."

Dani hung up and rushed inside. "Elena?" she called.

Cameron and Colin came running around a corner and nearly plowed right into her.

"Elena's sick, Mommy," Cameron blurted.

"Where is she?"

"In the kitchen." Colin took her hand and led her as if she didn't know the way.

Elena was sitting at the kitchen table with her head in her hands. She turned as Dani approached. She was extremely pale and there were dark circles under her eyes. "I'm so sorry."

"Please don't be sorry. These things happen. We just need to get you feeling better. Can I get you anything?"

Elena shook her head. "No. We had some ginger ale in the fridge. I'm just going to climb into bed and hope it goes away quickly."

"Yes. Of course. I have the boys. Just promise me that you'll buzz me if you need anything at all."

Elena slowly rose from the table, seeming unsteady. "I will."

Dani watched as Elena walked down the hall to the nanny suite and disappeared into her bedroom.

Dani dropped down to a crouch to talk to the boys. "What do you guys want to do for the rest of the day?" Between the sting, the hospital, and Cole's big news, Dani was quite frankly exhausted, but there would be no rest for the weary.

"We saw Mr. Cole's truck in the driveway. Is he here?" Cole asked, seeming terribly excited by the prospect.

"We looked everywhere," Cameron added.

"Is he coming over? Please say he's coming over."

Dani laughed quietly, but this was merely confirmation that she couldn't let Cole slip away this time. These boys loved him, and she did, too. She had to fight for him. She hadn't done that the first time, and perhaps that had been her biggest mistake. Everything might've been different now if she'd fought for him.

"No, Mr. Cole isn't here right now, but hopefully he'll come to get his truck in the next day or so. He's very busy right now." Dani didn't want the boys to worry, so she didn't mention that Cole was in the hospital. Dani still had no idea exactly how serious the news would be. She prayed that whatever it was, that she had the strength to help Cole with everything he was facing. Of course, she had no idea if he would even speak to her after she finally told him that the sweet boys standing before her were his sons.

Both boys' faces dropped in disappointment at the news that Cole was not around for fun. Dani felt the same way.

"We wanted him to see the swings and the monkey bars," Colin said.

"We were hoping he'd come play with us," Cameron added.

"Well, how about this? It's a beautiful day today. Why don't we do whatever Mr. Cole would want to do if he was here with us?"

"Swimming!" the boys proclaimed in unison.

Dani had little doubt that fun-loving, full-of-life Cole Sullivan would want to do exactly that. She choked back a few tears at how sad it was that he wasn't here. Making her all the more determined to finally come clean.

Eleven

Cole arrived back at his hospital room, only to learn that Dani was gone. His disappointment was immense. That was it. She'd taken off. She wanted no more of Cole Sullivan. Everything he'd feared as they wheeled him into that MRI room was right on the money. Well, maybe not everything. He still hadn't received his news from the doctor.

He got settled in his bed and took the pain medication the nurse offered. The headache had inexplicably gotten better during his test, but this stuff was fast acting and his agony was quickly fading. His physical misery might be disappearing quickly, but it was being upstaged by his state of mind—a harrowing mix of sadness, trepidation, and plain old worry. Between waiting for the doctor and wondering if Dani would ever speak to him again, things couldn't get any worse.

Out of nowhere, his brother Sam burst into his room. He was wearing his clothes from the ranch, cowboy hat and all. "I got here as fast as I could."

Cole sat up, wondering who in the hell thought up the design for hospital gowns. "How did you know I was here?"

"Dani called me." Sam sidled up to the bed and took a full survey of Cole. "She was worried. She didn't want you to be alone. But she had to leave. I think she needed to get to her boys."

Cole let out a deep sigh. Dani was clearly juggling a lot today and he'd had to go and heap one more thing on the pile by telling her about the glioma. At least she knew now. Come what may, the truth was out. "I'll have to thank her for that."

"Of course, it would've been nice if you'd called me or one of your other family members yourself. Were you just going to sit here and stew?"

Cole pressed his lips together tightly. "I'm thinking. And I needed to do it by myself."

"Thinking? Or worrying?" Sam reached for a small side chair and pulled it closer to Cole's bedside.

"At this point, I'm not sure I can separate the two. Every thought seems to come with a worry by default." Cole looked all around the room, hoping to hell this was not about to become his future. The doctor still hadn't come in to talk to him, and it was making him crazy. If he was dying, he just wanted to know so he could put his jeans and boots on and head back to the ranch, where he could at least keel over with a glass of bourbon in his hand while he sat out on the back terrace and watched the sun set. That was the way to go, not sitting in a mechanical bed wearing a sheet that opened in the back.

"Dani seems really worried, too."

"She does?" Cole couldn't decide if that was a good thing or a bad thing. "Tell me what she said."

Sam reared his head back and bugged his eyes. "I already told you. She didn't want you to be by yourself."

That wasn't enough to keep Cole going. That concern could certainly come accompanied with the sentiment that she never wanted to see him again. "Did she say what was going on with the boys? Are they okay?"

Sam shook his head. "She didn't say. And that was actually just a guess on my part. I think she said she needed to get home."

Now Cole felt even worse. Maybe Dani had simply wanted to get as far away from him as possible.

Just then there was a knock at the door and Dr. Lee came in with an entire team of people in white coats. Cole's stomach felt like it was down at his feet. Why would he need an army of doctors except to tell Cole that he was a goner?

"Mr. Sullivan, I brought a few of the residents with me today. I hope that's okay. If you prefer, they can wait out in the hall, but this is a teaching hospital. It's part of what we do."

Great. Cole had spent six years not wanting to

share this with the woman he loved. Now he had to share it with strangers. It didn't really matter, though. He'd already lost all sense of privacy, courtesy of the hospital gown. "Yeah. It's fine. Just tell me how long I have so I can get out of here. No offense, but I'm not a huge fan of this place."

Dr. Lee raised both eyebrows at Cole. "I hate to disappoint you, but you have exactly as long today as you did the day we last ran a scan. The glioma hasn't changed. At all."

Cole sat there for at least fifteen seconds, staring. Blinking. "Then why did I get that headache?" It had been the worst pain he'd ever endured, far more excruciating than broken ribs.

"I don't know. Could be any number of things. Stress is the most likely. You'd said you were on an airplane when it started, so the change in altitude could've built up pressure."

"So now what? More tests?"

"I'm on the fence, to be honest. It wouldn't be unreasonable to formally admit you and monitor you until tomorrow morning."

"What would that entail?"

"You sitting in that bed and the nurse checking on you every two hours."

Cole threw back the covers. "How about I just call you if the headache comes back?"

Dr. Lee stepped forward and held up a hand. "Hold on a minute. Are you really that anxious to get out of here?"

Cole nearly laughed. "Yes. I am." *I've got a woman I need to talk to.*

Dr. Lee pressed his lips into a thin line. "Okay. We will release you. Plus you have to promise me you will call me the instant you get a headache this bad again."

Cole held up his hand. "I promise."

"You're still going to need to wait for the paperwork to clear. Which could take a few hours."

Hospital bureaucracy—Cole hated it. But he did need to look on the bright side. The glioma hadn't changed. It hadn't grown. In six years, nothing inside his head had changed. But in less than two weeks, Dani had not only turned around his thinking, she'd gotten his heart beating again. She'd reminded him just how badly he wanted to be here. She'd shown him how good it was to be alive. Especially when you have someone to love.

"I'll have the nurses get your paperwork going. Plan on coming to see me during clinic hours in six months or so. I'll have them send you an appointment reminder. And call me if anything changes."

With that, the doctor and crew left, meaning Sam and Cole were now alone.

"That's good news, buddy," Sam declared, rising up out of his seat. "Now you just need to get the rest of your life straightened out."

"What exactly is that supposed to mean?"

"I asked Dani if you two were back together."

Cole sometimes couldn't believe his brother's

willingness to say or ask anything, but today, he was glad for it. "And what did she say?"

"She said she wasn't sure. She said you had some things to work out."

A heavy sigh left Cole's lips. "I need to finish telling her everything about our breakup. What I was thinking. I need to explain myself. I hardly got it out of my mouth before they whisked me out the door."

"Only she can say what her reaction will be, but judging by my conversation with her, I'd say she'll definitely listen."

"Well, that's something." Cole sat back, trying not to play out the conversation in his head. These things weren't always predictable with Dani.

"I'm sensing there's something else that's still bothering you."

Cole didn't know how to bring up this subject with Sam, so he certainly wasn't ready to do so with Dani. Maybe simply talking about it would help him sort this out a bit in his head. "I want to talk to her about her boys. Cameron and Colin." Just saying their names made for this tug right in the center of his chest.

"What about them, exactly?"

Cole realized how crazy this was going to sound. "Have you noticed how much they look like me? Especially Colin."

"I've only seen them for a few minutes the day you had them over to swim in the pool. But yes, it did make me wonder. She hasn't told you who their father is?"

"No. And I haven't asked. She's a single mom. It's incredibly insensitive."

"Of course. There's no good way to bring it up."

"Exactly." At least Sam seemed to understand how he was feeling. "But there's this feeling in my gut that says they're my boys. I have to know. I just need to know if I'm off base."

"Will that change the way you feel about Dani? Could you forgive a woman for keeping your children a secret for that long?"

Cole ran his hands through his hair and looked his brother square in the eye. "I don't want to waste any more time in my life, Sam. I have to forgive her. My heart won't survive it if we can't find a way to make it work. One half of that job is mine, which means I have to forgive."

"And how will you feel if they aren't yours?"

Cole shrugged. "Honestly? I don't know if it would make a lick of difference. I'd still adore them. I'd still want to be in their lives."

Sam grinned sideways. "You know, I watched you that day in the pool with the boys. You were having so much fun. And I've seen you with Dani, It's like you didn't skip a beat. If ever there was a family just waiting to be put together, it's the four of you."

Cole smiled and nodded slowly, looking out the window of his room. Another beautiful, sunny day in Royal—clear blue sky and a few fluffy clouds. It was the perfect day for turning life around. And now that he'd had the chance to talk out his feelings with

Sam, he felt all the more ready to do the same with Dani. Everything else he'd have to put in her hands.

Cole changed into his regular clothes while Sam went outside to make a phone call. Once the paperwork was complete and Cole got the all clear, Sam insisted on driving him straight out to the ranch. "I don't feel great about you driving yet. We can get your truck from Dani's later," he'd said. As soon as he dropped Cole off at the main house, he left. "I need to check on some things in the barn. I'll see you later."

Cole headed straight upstairs and immediately climbed into the shower to wash off that hospital smell and hopefully start to feel a bit more human. With a clean pair of jeans and T-shirt, and his mind mostly straight, he knew he had to reach out to Dani. Maybe she could come over tonight so they could talk. It might take hours, but they had to arrive at some understanding. He hoped like hell that at the end of all of it, they concluded that they should be together. He wasn't sure he could handle the heartbreak of the alternative.

He bounded downstairs in search of his cell phone, which he'd left on the kitchen counter. As soon as he pressed Dani's number, he could've sworn he heard laughter, and not just any laughter. Kids. *The boys.* He walked into the living room with the phone pressed to his ear. The call was still ringing as he opened the front door. The boys made a beeline for his front steps. He hadn't imagined this. This was real.

"Hello?" Dani said into the phone, a tentative grin on her face as she climbed out of the minivan. "I was hoping we could talk."

"Good. Me, too," he answered.

"I'll hang up now." She closed the driver's side door and started heading for him, but he couldn't get a handle on what she was thinking. There was part of him that still worried she was here to tell him she just couldn't get past everything he'd kept from her. "How are you feeling?"

"A lot better now that you're here." Cole was slow to tuck his phone into his pocket, even after she'd hung up. He didn't want to risk wasting a second of their conversation, even when the boys were now hanging on him, tugging on his shirt and begging to go see Gentry.

Dani arrived at the base of the staircase. The late-afternoon sun lit up the side of her face, making her somehow even more beautiful than usual. "Do you have some time for me?"

"Always." Out of the corner of his eye, Cole saw Sam walking out of the stable and heading for the house. Cole crouched down. "Hey, Colin and Cameron, your mom and I have something to talk about. Do you want to spend some time with Sam and see how the new foal is doing? She still doesn't have a name yet. I was hoping you two could think of one."

The boys turned and saw Sam, then tore off down the stairs. Cole followed them. "I'll be right back," he said to Dani, then caught up with his brother.

"Do you mind taking the boys to see the foal? I was thinking that they might be able to give her a name."

Sam swiped his sunglasses from his face. "Time to straighten things out with their mom?"

"You know it. This could take a while. I've got a lot to apologize for."

Sam clapped his brother on the back. "You need to stop being so hard on yourself."

"A man messes up, he needs to take responsibility."

"True. You did mess up." Sam glanced behind him. The boys were waiting patiently at the stable doors. "I'd better go catch up with those two."

"Thank you." Cole watched as his brother sidled down to Cameron and Colin. He felt a tug on his heart just looking at those boys. They were his. He knew it. But he sure as heck wanted to hear Dani say it.

He turned back to the house and there Dani was, sitting on the top step of the porch. The breeze blew her glossy dark hair from her shoulders, and the sun was now lighting up the other side of her beautiful face. He'd be lying if he said he didn't want this to be his entire life—Dani and the boys, on the ranch. It was all he wanted.

Dani stood when she spotted him heading back. She spoke as soon as he was within spitting distance. "I don't care what you're facing, Cole. I don't care what's going on. I'm here for you."

He climbed the stairs, stopping on the step below her. "I appreciate that. A lot." Even though that made him feel a bit better, his heart was still pounding in his chest.

"I won't let you push me away again. No matter what the doctor told you today."

He managed a bit of a smile. In the midst of all this turmoil, he'd gotten good news. "The glioma hasn't changed. They think the headache was brought on by stress and the pressure changes in the plane."

Dani let out a huge exhale and pressed her hand to her chest. "Oh, thank God. I'm so relieved to hear that."

She peered up into his eyes and took his hand. "And I have something that I need to tell you. Something I should have told you a long time ago that I don't want to keep inside anymore. Colin and Cameron are your sons."

He scanned her face as she waited for his response. She was so nervous and uncertain it nearly broke his heart. "They're mine? Really?" He couldn't have disguised the excitement in his voice if he'd wanted to. He'd been unprepared for how good it was going to feel to get this news.

She unleashed a relieved smile. "I never should've kept that from you, and I'm sorry. But I was sure you wanted nothing to do with me, ever."

Cole let her words wash over him, soaking them up. This was confirmation that he had no more time to waste. There was a whole lot of life waiting for him, and he didn't want to spend another minute of it worrying about what might be. "The glioma is why I ended things. Every minute you spent taking care of me felt like confirmation that you deserved a long life with someone who could give that to you. I couldn't promise you that I would be around."

Dani's eyes were so soft and caring. It was like he could see how big her heart was. "So what's the prognosis now?" She sat back down on the top step and Cole joined her, taking her hand.

He launched into the technical side of his condition, or at least the parts he could remember. "I still feel a little bit like a ticking time bomb, but Sam and I had a good talk at the hospital. I'm sorry I didn't have the chance to tell you more before they whisked me off for my MRI. Everything happened so fast."

"It's okay. I understand so much more now. You were in an incredibly tight spot." There were tears in her eyes when she looked at him. "And I'm so sorry you didn't feel like you could tell me. That's why you told me there was another woman, isn't it? That's why you didn't answer my letter."

He squeezed her hand tightly. "I need you to know that both of those things were hard for me. Very hard. I thought it was for your own good."

"You can do some really stupid things, Cole Sullivan." She added a sweet smile, just to let him know she was giving him a hard time for fun.

"Yeah. I realize that now. Being protective isn't always my best quality."

"No. I think it's one of your best." Dani cast her sights off in the distance, holding on to his hand just as tightly he was holding on to hers. In that single touch he knew exactly how badly they needed each other. "I came close to telling you about the boys when I wrote that letter. That might've changed everything."

"It absolutely would've changed everything. Why didn't you?"

"Because I wanted you to want to be with me out of love, not because you felt obligated."

"I never stopped loving you, Dani. And it would've been impossible for me to not feel obligated. Even if we didn't work out, I still would've been their daddy."

She nodded. "I can see now that it wasn't the right call, but at the time, I couldn't see another way. Those boys are the best thing that has ever happened to me, but they've also been my greatest trial."

The thought of Dani doing the work of both parents for all these years made it hard for Cole to get past the lump in his throat. Talk about his male ego getting in the way—he really hated the thought of not living up to his responsibilities, even if he hadn't known they'd existed. Regardless of how things played out with Dani, he had a lot to make up for. "Because you were raising them on your own."

"Well, there's that, but that's not the real reason. It's been hard because I had to look into their eyes every day and see the face of the man I loved. It was like being haunted by the ghost of Cole Sullivan."

Cole had to laugh, but it wasn't funny. This was something born out of deep frustration with himself. "I think I've been living with that same ghost. I was so sure I was going to die that I think I stopped living. But that all changed the night you showed up on this porch in that ridiculously sexy red dress. It was like you brought me back to life that night."

"I turned you down that night. And I called you a mistake."

"Sometimes it's the cruelest things that remind you you're alive." He turned to her, studying her sweet face and those tempting lips. He couldn't wait another second to kiss her. He wanted to start their new chapter right here and right now. "But for right now, I'd like to go for a good reminder that I'm still here."

Twelve

Sitting there on Cole's font porch, Dani's mind was running a million miles a minute, thinking about the suffering he'd done all alone, when they could have been together. A less charitable woman might be berating him right now, but Dani was done with being mad. She just wanted to move on with the man she loved.

He pulled her into his arms and placed the softest kiss on her lips. It felt like a new beginning, a hello, a beautiful fresh start. It was exactly what they both needed so badly. It left her heart pulsing like crazy, full of good feelings that had been gone for far too long.

Cole gently pulled his lips away and rested his forehead against hers, but he was still holding on tight. "I never stopped loving you, Dani. Not even for a minute. I just had to protect you. Now I can see how foolish that was."

She gripped both sides of his face and looked up into his incredible blue eyes. For as tough as Cole was, his eyes had always revealed kindness. They were the way in. "I'm ready to put that all behind us. I think we could both use a fresh start."

"As long as you understand there are no guarantees."

She could hardly believe he was still couching this. "I hate to break this to you, but there are no guarantees with any man, especially not one foolish enough to want to run around and chase bad guys like Richard Lowell."

Cole laughed quietly and smiled. "I'm sorry, but I don't know any other way. There's just this part of me that will always want to find justice."

She turned her hand and tenderly brushed the side of his face with the backs of her fingers. "I know. That's part of what I've always loved about you. Just like my daddy."

"I wish I could've known him."

Dani choked back the weight of Cole's statement. "He would've loved you. I think the boys got that same justice-seeking bug. You already saw how riled up they get if one of them gets more ice cream than the other."

"Ice cream is serious stuff." His head moved slow as molasses as he nodded, like it was all sinking in. "Wow. Is this real? Am I really a daddy?"

She clapped him on the thigh. "It's really real. And I think it's time that we tell them. If you're ready."

"I think we both know I'm done with waiting."

If only Cole knew what a big leap that was for Dani. She'd spent the years trying to teach the boys that it didn't matter who their daddy was, that they had her and that was all that was important. But the reality was it did matter—Cole was a good man and he wanted a relationship with his boys. He wanted to be a part of their lives, she wanted the same, and she already knew they would welcome him.

Sam and the boys were heading up from the stables, Colin and Cameron running so fast that they were kicking up dirt. They ran Dani ragged some days. Now they could start spending time with their father, and hopefully he could help to wear them out a little bit. Sam waved at Dani and Cole, then headed off behind the house. He must have sensed that they would need their time together.

As the boys ran up the stairs, they were a flurry of news and announcements.

"We gave the foal a name," Cameron said.

"What did you decide on?"

"Dottie. After Great-Aunt Dot," Colin explained, as if the name required clarification.

Dani smiled wide. They were so impossibly sweet. "I think that sounds like a wonderful name."

"Is that okay with you, Mr. Cole?" Cameron asked.

"Absolutely. I approve."

"Oh, good." Colin seemed legitimately worried.

"There's only one thing," Cole added. "I'd like it if you boys started calling me something other than Mr. Cole."

Dani's gaze connected with Cole's, and she knew the moment had arrived. She pulled both boys close. "I have something important to tell you. Do you remember when we talked about how one day you might meet your father?"

Colin was busy putting two and two together, but Cameron seemed to catch on right away. His mouth flew open and he looked back and forth between Cole and Dani. "Is he?"

Dani nodded. "Yes, honey. Mr. Sullivan and I were in love a long time ago. And that's when you two came along. Mr. Sullivan is your daddy."

"You are?" Colin, ever the skeptic, stepped up to Cole and placed his hands on his knee, scrutinizing his face. "Are you spoofing us?"

"I would never spoof you about something so important. You boys have the same freckles as Mr. Sullivan and everything. You don't get those from me," Dani said.

"Actually," Cole interjected, "I have some photos inside the house of me as a little boy. Maybe we can get a drink of water and take a look at those."

"I think that sounds like a wonderful idea," Dani said, amazed how the boys were taking this all in stride, although she probably shouldn't be surprised. They'd loved Cole from the moment they met him, and they were both so sweet natured and accepting, it only made sense that this news would be well received.

That said, she knew they'd have hurdles to jump at some point. Undoubtedly, both boys would have questions about the future, about what would happen and how this all might shake out. She had to prepare for that, which meant another big discussion with Cole.

She followed Cole and the boys inside, and they settled in the living room with a photo album and ice water, while Dani decided to make a pitcher of lemonade. When she returned to the living room, the vision took her breath away—Cole sitting on that big leather sofa of his, Colin on one side and Cameron on the other. The boys were still so small, their feet hardly reached the edge of those deep seat cushions. They were looking through a photo album.

"Now, this is me and Sam at one of our first state fairs, showing goats. I'm guessing I was eight and he was five," Cole said.

"Did you win?" Colin asked.

Cole shook his head. "Nope. Competition was steep. But we learned a lot. I guess that's the most important part."

"I made lemonade," Dani said, setting down the pitcher and glasses on the coffee table. The boys practically leaped off the sofa to get theirs.

Cole scooted to the edge of his seat, and took a sip, breaking down Dani's defenses with a single smoldering gaze. Not that she had any need for defenses right now.

"Mommy, why didn't you tell us about Mr. Cole earlier?" Colin asked.

"Hold on one second, because I do want to hear Mommy's answer, but I think the foal isn't the only one on the ranch who could use a new name." The boys turned to him, their eyes wide with curiosity. "I realize this is all brand-new, and you don't have to call me anything you aren't comfortable with, but if you don't want to call me Dad or Daddy, or maybe Pa, at least just call me Cole." He dropped his chin and looked at both boys, appraising their response.

Colin turned back to Dani. "Mommy, why didn't you tell us about Daddy sooner?"

A satisfied grin crossed Cole's face and he cocked both eyebrows, laughing to himself. "I guess I'm Daddy."

"Indeed you are," Dani replied. She turned her attention to the boys so she could answer Colin's question. "Grown-ups make mistakes, too. This was a big mistake I made, but your dad and I had an argument once and that was the start of it. I'm sorry about that. Truly sorry. But I hope you can both forgive me."

The boys both smiled and smothered her in hugs and kisses. It was the absolute best part of being a mom. A close second would be seeing them with Cole just now. Everything was right.

"Boys, I was a big part of this mistake, too. Your mom was doing her best to protect you."

Dani appreciated Cole's willingness to shoulder some of the blame, although she was simply tired of pointing fingers. "The important thing right now is for you two to spend some time with your daddy and get to know him even better."

"Would you like to sleep over here at the ranch tonight?" Cole asked.

The boys erupted into a chorus of affirmation.

"I mean, if it's okay with Mom," he added.

She knew exactly what he was up to with that leading inflection of his voice, and she had to say that she was board. Sharing a bed tonight would be the perfect way to top off their reconciliation. Maybe in the morning, they could begin the discussion on how to merge their lives and households.

"Of course it's okay with me. I want us to spend as much time together as possible. Elena's still resting, but I'll run back to the house and pick up some clothes."

"Mommy, can you bring our bathing suits?" Colin climbed back up on the couch and snuggled in closer to Cole.

"Does that mean you want to go swimming?" Cole asked.

Colin looked up at Cole with all earnestness. Dani could only admire them—the spitting image of each other, and they finally knew why.

"Can we? Please?" Colin asked.

Cole put his arm around his son and pulled him closer. "We can do whatever you want, buddy."

As soon as she got home, Dani went to check on Elena, rapping softly on her bedroom door.

"Come in," Elena said.

Dani stepped inside. "How's the patient?"

Elena was sitting up in bed, reading. "Much better. I think it was something I ate. I should be back to normal tomorrow."

"Good. I'm glad to hear that."

"Where are the boys? I don't hear them, so I assume they aren't home."

"They're actually out at the ranch with Cole. We're all staying over there tonight."

"Oh, really?" Elena arched a brow and turned to Dani. "What's the latest?"

Dani told her everything about how she and Cole had both finally divulged their secrets.

"A glioma. That's serious stuff."

Dani nodded. "It is. But I told him we'll just face it together."

Elena smiled. "That's great. It seems like things have been worked out."

Now that the high of her reconciliation with Cole was starting to die down, reality was starting to settle in. Everything wasn't worked out, but Dani had to be hopeful. They had a lot to decide. Logic said that they would move in together. Blend their lives. Get married. Dani knew she needed to take this one step at a time. After all, they'd moved beyond two huge obstacles to find forgiveness. If they could do that, everything else should be a piece of cake.

"We're beginning the process of putting things back together. It's going to take some time to figure everything out."

"I don't need to worry about my job, do I? I hate asking the question. You've done so much for me."

Elena's face was painted with worry, and Dani felt as though the bottom of her stomach might drop.

"There is absolutely nothing to worry about. Nothing. I need you to be there for the boys. Nothing about that has changed."

The corners of her mouth turned into a smile. "Oh, thank God. I was worried."

Dani went and sat on the edge of Elena's bed. "Are you kidding? I couldn't have gotten through the last five years without you. And the boys love you. I would never take you away from them. Now get some sleep. I'll be home in the morning. I have to go in to the Glass House tomorrow afternoon to talk menu changes with the staff, and I told them I'd be there for tomorrow night's dinner service. Between that crazy trip to California and everything with Cole, I've spent too little time in the trenches. I need to put my chef's coat back on and get to work."

"Well, just keep me posted. I'll be at the house if you need anything."

Less than an hour later, Dani returned with a duffel of clothes for her and the boys, along with toothbrushes and other essentials. Cole helped the boys change into their bathing suits while Dani left their bag in the guest room where the boys would sleep and took her own things to Cole's master suite, directly across the hall.

Dani headed back downstairs. Cole had left the French doors leading out to the backyard wide-open, ushering in warm breezes and the sound of big splashes and delighted squeals. She stepped out onto the flagstone patio, which was already darkened by plenty of water. Cole and the boys had wasted no time. He was in the shallow end with them, hoisting Colin up high and tossing him into deeper water. Colin swam to the edge and shook the water from his face while his brother took a turn. Cole waited until Cameron swam to safety, then approached her, wading to the side where she was standing. If ever a man was poetry in motion, Cole was, especially while the droplets of water on his chest and shoulders glistened in the sun and his aviator sunglasses sparkled.

"You gonna put on your bathing suit and get in with us?" He reached out and touched her ankle with the tip of his finger. How the man could turn her on with a single touch, especially when she had so much on her mind, she didn't know.

"I am. I was just enjoying the scenery."

Cole's eyebrows bounced. "Oh, yeah? Well, there's plenty of time to enjoy that later tonight."

As planned, the instant the boys were sound asleep, Dani and Cole were in his room, door locked, hands all over each other and clothes coming off faster than Dani could keep up with. It was no surprise things boiled over so quickly—they'd spent their entire evening together exchanging heated, smoldering glances while there was absolutely nothing they could do until the boys went to bed.

They kissed, tongues winding. They fell into a naked heap on the bed. Cole was quick to roll Dani to her back and start kissing her neck. She wanted him so badly she could hardly see straight.

"I'm so glad we worked everything out," Dani managed before Cole claimed her mouth with another hot, wet kiss.

"Me, too." Cole gripped her ribcage and drew her nipple between his warm lips, gently tugging.

Dani moaned softly, digging her fingertips into Cole's shoulders. "I want you, Cole. Now." She spread her legs and watched as she fell under his gaze. She'd never felt so wanted *and* loved. What a wonderful combination.

As he drove inside, Dani raised her hips to meet him. They fell into their rhythm effortlessly, just as they'd managed to fall back into sync with their lives. Cole's eyes were dark with desire, his breaths ragged. Dani's peak was approaching, so she wrapped her legs tightly around Cole's hips, muscling him closer. He got the message loud and clear, bearing down in exactly the right now. A few forceful thrusts were all it took before Dani was unraveling in his arms. Cole followed with his climax, kissing her deeply as the pleasure shuddered through his strong body.

He rolled to Dani's side, but was quick to pull her close. He tenderly brushed her messy hair from her forehead. His was lightly glistening with sweat.

"I love you so much, Dani. We can rebuild a life together."

Dani smiled and burrowed her face in Cole's chest, inhaling his warm smell. "I love you so much, too. And I know we can. We can do anything now."

* * *

After a blissful night in each other's arms, Cole and Dani awoke to the sound of tiny frantic knocks at his bedroom door. It sounded like there was a woodpecker out there. "Mommy? Can we come in?" the boys asked.

"It must be seven if they're up," she said to Cole, getting out of bed to open the door.

"How do you know it's seven?"

"The boys know not to bother me before then unless it's an emergency."

"I guess I have a lot to learn." Cole, too, got out of bed and joined Dani at the door. He crouched down for the boys. "Hey, guys. Do you remember how I showed you the other day how to feed the chickens? Do you think you could go do that for me?"

Cameron nodded so fast Dani thought his little head might pop off. "Yes, please."

"Go put some clothes on," she said. "We'll meet you downstairs for breakfast when you're done."

"Okay." With that, the boys tore off.

Cole straightened and shot Dani a quizzical look. "Was that okay? Is there some morning routine I don't know about?"

She kissed his cheek. "Not today. You did perfectly."

Cole went off to change and Dani padded downstairs to put on a pot of coffee, doing some prep for pancakes while it brewed. She took a mug into the living room and looked out over the backyard, with the miles of ranch land stretching out beyond it. She wasn't sure she could feel more fortunate than she did right now.

The front door opened, and in waltzed Cameron and Colin. "The chickens were super hungry."

"And how about my boys? You two up for pancakes and bacon?" Dani asked.

As with most things, they responded with great enthusiasm.

Dani went to work while Cole sent the boys to wash their hands and poured them some orange juice. When they returned from the bathroom, Cole got them seated at the kitchen island. He walked over as Dani was flipping the pancakes and pulling the bacon from the skillet.

"Can I help?" Cole wrapped his arms around her waist, pulling her against his long body and kissing her neck softly.

Dani nearly had to grab the kitchen counter to remain standing. "Your timing is impeccable. We're ready to eat."

They got the boys' plates ready, but Dani stopped Cole before he delivered them. "Do you have a few minutes to talk this morning? After breakfast?"

"Probably. I'm waiting for a call from the FBI agents. They've been scouting out a location where they think Rich might have his stash hidden."

"Okay. Well, there are some things I'd like to discuss about the future."

Cole's phone rang right on cue. "I'm sorry. I have to take this." He wandered off into the living room, leaving her with the boys.

"Are we staying here again tonight?" Cameron asked before putting nearly half a pancake in his mouth.

That was exactly the sort of question she'd wanted to avoid, or at least have an answer for. "I'm not quite sure, honey. I think we might stay at our house tonight. I have to go to work and I think Daddy does, too. There's no preschool today, so I'll take you home to spend the day with Elena."

"What about tomorrow?" Colin loved to dig deeper.

"I'm not sure yet, sweetie. But don't worry. We'll get it worked out."

Cole tucked his phone into his back pocket and walked back into the kitchen. "I'm so sorry. I have to go. They need me for this."

Dani nodded. She understood the importance of it, and she wanted Rich to be caught just as badly as Cole did. "No problem."

"We can talk later. I promise." He took her hand and raised it to his lips, flashing those brilliant blue eyes of his.

Tingles raced over the surface of her skin. She knew they would work every last silly detail out. They'd come too far to accept anything less. "I love you, Cole."

Cole pulled her into his arms and placed a soft kiss on her lips. "I love you, too."

Thirteen

Based on intel gathered before and after the sting to catch Sheriff Orson, the team was racing to find Rich's stash. Or so Cole hoped. There had been so many setbacks in this investigation, it was hard to bank on much, but Cole was hopeful. Having Dani back in his life had helped him turn around his thinking. Hope had been missing for too long.

"You feeling good about this?" Will had met Cole at the TCC and jumped into his car with him. He really wanted to be there for this, and it was hard to blame him.

Special Agents Bird and Stanton were leading the way in an unmarked car, with Sheriff Battle behind them. Everyone was keeping their distance to avoid the appearance of a caravan. They didn't want to announce their arrival or risk anyone being tipped off, especially as they ventured farther into the rural reaches of the county, where traffic jams did not happen.

Cole sucked in a deep breath. "I am. I don't want to jinx it or anything, but I know we are closing in on Rich. Today we should find another piece of this puzzle. A big one."

"Well, good. That makes me glad. I just want this to be over with so I can get on with my life."

"I know. Things have been on hold for you for too long. But don't worry, Will. We'll get him. Your name will be cleared, and hopefully Rich will spend the rest of his life in a very small jail cell." Just saying those things reminded Cole that there was an awful lot on the line here and he'd better not screw any of it up. Whether or not Will could move on from this nightmare and live a normal life depended on Cole. The same went for Megan, Savannah and Aaron. A lot of people were counting on him.

"You've been a real friend to me through all of this," Will said. "I'm not sure how I could ever repay you."

"You're already paying me. I'm just doing my job."

Will laughed quietly. "I know. But when your life has been turned completely upside down, it's nice to have some help turning it right side up. You've been on my side this whole time."

Cole nodded, taking in Will's kind words and letting them tumble around in his head for a bit. If Cole were honest, he'd turned his own life upside down the day he'd banished Dani. Thank goodness she'd resurfaced and helped him see the error of his ways. "I appreciate that. Truly. I just want to get the TCC their money back and make things right for you and for Jason's family, too. They've suffered too much at Rich's hand."

"I really want that for Megan. Hell, I need it for her. She deserves a new beginning. At the very least."

Cole wasn't the type to come out and ask a guy about his love life, but there had definitely been sparks between Megan and Will at Jason's memorial service. Judging by the passionate tone of Will's voice, there might be a real romance brewing. "Of course. She deserves that new beginning so she can move on and live a happy life."

"Yes. I want her to be happy."

Cole took a gander at the GPS on his dash. "That's our turnoff up ahead. We're almost there." The site was about fifteen miles outside town, up a long and twisting dusty road. From the information they'd been able to gather, the property had been unoccupied and unused for years, tucked away in a forgotten corner of the county. The incline was getting steeper, Cole's truck shifting into a lower gear as the tires of the car ahead of them kicked up more dirt.

Cole took the final bend, a near hairpin turn. The road narrowed and pitched sharply downward, now suspiciously covered in fresh gravel. Someone had done some work out here recently, possibly to make it easier to get a truck in and out. The hair on the back of his neck stood up straight. They were in the right place. He knew it. Ahead, down in a flat gully, sat a tired ramshackle house with a wraparound porch and faded gray clapboards. The windows were boarded up, and a rusty No Trespassing sign hung from a metal cattle gate leaning against a rotting post.

Cole parked his truck next to the FBI vehicle, and he and Will climbed out. Bird and Stanton were arguing like an old married couple, which was par for the course for them. Battle's car pulled up right behind them. Cole had considered obtaining a warrant to search the property, but Bird had done some digging and learned that this was a foreclosure that had been on the books with a bank in Albuquerque for more than ten years.

Leave it to Rich to find the one place in Royal that neither Cole nor the sheriff knew about, a place that for all intents and purposes didn't matter to anyone. For that reason, and since this was a fact-finding mission where they intended to leave no trace that they'd been on-site, they'd decided to forgo the warrant. Rich had managed to be a step ahead of them at too many points in this investigation. They couldn't afford a single mistake now that they were closing in on him.

"Cole, you leading us in?" Sheriff Battle asked.

Cole smiled, securing his bulletproof vest, which was just a precaution at this point. Agents coordinated by Bird had had eyes on this location for more than twenty-four hours and hadn't seen anyone come or go, so they were reasonably sure it was unoccupied. "I'd be happy to." He led the way down the steep drive, his boots crunching in the gravel. They advanced on the house, and Sheriff Battle and his deputy ran around to the back. Cole stepped up on to the front porch. The decking boards were so dry and brittle it felt as if his boot might go straight through them.

He pounded on the wood door, which was far sturdier than the porch floor. In fact, Cole was pretty sure it had been reinforced. If there was something inside this house, the owner did not want it found.

No answer came. Sheriff Battle radioed that there was an unboarded window on the back and that they couldn't see anyone inside. Cole pounded one more time, then got out his kit to pick the lock. It was the best way to keep their visit a secret.

Like magic, the door popped open. Cole immediately saw that it *had* been reinforced with heavy-gauge steel. The place was empty—old wood floors, more dust and cobwebs than a bad haunted house. Cole trailed across the front room and rapped on the window glass. Thick. And hazy, although he suspected not from time or grime. It was bulletproof. Further evidence that something was here, and whatever it was, it was big.

Stanton walked back into the room. "The house is clear."

"All right, then. Now we really look," Cole said.

The team searched every square inch, rapping on walls, listening for dead spots. It wasn't until Cole drove the heel of his boot into the floor of the kitchen pantry that he figured out there was a false panel. "Sheriff," he called, dropping down to his knees and feeling around the perimeter near the baseboards. "Bird. Stanton. I think I found something."

Sheriff Battle rushed into the room, followed closely by the FBI agents. "Let's see what we got."

With the help of a crowbar, Cole was able to lift the panel, which was cut perfectly to fit the space. What he saw under the floor was almost too much to believe—bar after bar of solid gold. "Bingo," Cole said. Vindication sure felt good.

"Hoo, doggy," Sheriff Battle said, looking over Cole's shoulder and down into the carefully constructed metal compartments hanging between the floor joists. This gold had been well hidden. Just not quite well enough.

"There's no way we can confiscate this now. It's just too much. We'd have to bring in much bigger trucks and a crew. And get that warrant." Cole's brain was in overdrive as his eyes pored over the glistening gold bars, mulling over the questions and possible answers. Was this the money missing from the TCC and Will's accounts? Was it Rich's plan to use this money after he faked his own death and killed Jason in the process? If so, Rich had to be coming back soon. What more damage could he possibly do? They not only had to catch him soon, this was the best place to do it. "We can be damn sure that Rich will come back out here for this. There's no way he's just going to leave this behind, especially if he's figured out we're on to him. It's only a matter of time before he tries to get to this and hightail it out of the country, probably back to Mexico."

"Agreed. I think that's our best course of action," Stanton said. "We'll lock everything up and request a pair of agents out here to keep an eye on it around the clock. Nobody will be able to touch this without us knowing about it."

Cole was a bit disappointed in that part of the plan, since it only meant more waiting, but he reminded himself that his patience would ultimately be rewarded. With the help of Sheriff Battle, he got the panel back into place and they left the house in the same condition as when they'd arrived.

Cole said his goodbyes to Battle, Bird and Stanton, promising that they would have a call soon to discuss their plan to get Rich out to this house to retrieve his gold. He then drove Will back to his car at the TCC.

"Thanks for letting me ride along today," Will said. "At least I know we're one step closer to catching Rich."

"Every step forward is a good one." He clapped Will on the shoulder. "I'll talk to you soon."

"Absolutely."

Cole waited until Will's car started up, then he got his own show on the road, racing back to the ranch as quickly as traffic laws allowed. He was filthy after running around at that old house, and that did not mesh with his plans for this evening. He bounded up the stairs when he got home, rushed inside and turned on the shower. It took a few minutes to wash away the grime, but he was focused.

As he looked at himself in the mirror and shaved his stubble away, he rehearsed a few things in his head. *I love you so much. I can't lose you again.* Just the thought of saying those words put a lump in his throat. He hoped to hell he could actually do this. With no time to overthink it, he dressed in a pair of jeans and a clean shirt. Before he ran out the door, he grabbed the most important piece of this puzzle— still residing in his sock drawer, at the very back, tucked away for six years. The ring. He popped open the box to make sure it was still there and indeed it was, just as sparkly and lovely as the woman he hoped would wear it. Now to get his answer.

His heart flip-flopped in his chest as he climbed into his truck and headed over to Dani's. The thought of what he was going to ask her made his hands clammy. A bit ironic considering he hadn't felt a lick of nervousness breaking into a criminal's stash of gold a few hours ago. But he hadn't waited as long to do that as he'd waited for this. Much more than the six years they'd been apart. He shouldn't be so unsure of himself, but if Dani could be relied on for anything, it was the unexpected. If she said no, he wasn't sure he could survive, but he couldn't think like that. Not now. He'd lost his precious family once, and there was no way he was going to lose them again.

Dani drove home just after 10:00 p.m., exhausted. It'd been an amazing night of business at the restaurant and everything had gone great, but she'd forgotten how hard it was on her body to be in the kitchen during the dinner rush.

She was struck by the thought that kept cycling through her head—she wished she were going home to Cole. She wanted nothing more than to share a glass of wine with him, fall into his arms, make love with him and slip into blissful sleep. That was all she needed—the simplest, but most beautiful of things in life, with Cole.

She was also listening loudly to her heart right now, which was whispering to her, pointing out that what Dani really wanted was marriage. She wanted to go home to Cole every night. Not just this one.

As she pulled into her neighborhood and turned on to her street, she smiled to herself when she realized that she could be the one to ask Cole to marry her. She could look into his beautiful blue eyes, tell him she loved him and pop the question. Would it be the craziest thing in the world? She did love the idea of catching Cole off guard. It would be an amazing story for their grandchildren.

When she approached her house, Cole's hulking truck in the driveway was unmistakable. Her already present smile grew wider. She did get to come home to Cole. Or at least see him for a little bit. Now she was feeling decidedly less exhausted.

As soon as she opened the garage door, things got confusing. The minivan was gone, which was not right for this time of night. Were the boys home? What about Elena? She parked her car and turned off the ignition, rushing into the house. It was incredibly quiet. Almost too quiet. "Hello?" Her voice echoed in the back hall off the kitchen. She got no response, so she hurried upstairs.

The boys' bedroom door was closed, and sure enough, when she opened it, they were sound asleep in their beds. Elena would never leave them alone, so what in the heck had happened to the minivan? And if Cole's truck was here, where was he? She tiptoed in and straightened their blankets, kissed them each on top of their heads, and quietly closed the door.

She headed into her bedroom and jumped when she saw what was waiting for her—Cole, asleep on her bed. He was reclining on several pillows propped up against the headboard, a book resting on his chest. The bedside table lamp was on, casting him in a warm glow. She couldn't contain her grin as she approached him. He was so handsome it nearly sucked the breath right out of her. Good God, she loved him. That much she didn't have to worry about ever again.

She perched on the edge of the bed, sitting right next to his leg. She gently picked up the book, but that was enough to get him to stir.

"Hey. You're home," he said, looking sleepy and more than a little sexy.

"I am. What are you doing here?" She rubbed his arm gently, feeling so lucky that the dream scenario she'd cooked up in the car might actually happen.

"I came over as soon as I finished up my work stuff. I wanted to spend some time with the boys.

We swam for a while, and then I took them out for burgers for dinner."

"Oh, yum."

"We had french fries and shakes and everything."

Dani nodded. Cole's mischievous side was definitely one of his more appealing qualities. "Healthy."

"It wasn't. But it was delicious." He unleashed his electric grin.

"Where's the minivan?"

"I told Elena I had everything under control. She went to a movie, I think."

"So what happened after dinner?"

"We came home and I gave the boys a bath and read them stories and put them to bed."

Dani didn't cry easily, but she felt that single tear leak from the corner of her eye, and she knew it was futile to try to stop it. Another tear followed. And another.

"Why are you crying?" Cole sat up and put his hand on her shoulder, seeming truly concerned. "Oh my God. I completely forgot I was supposed to call you. I was so wrapped up in work, and then I wanted to get over here to see the boys, and I don't know what happened. Time just sort of got away from me. I'm so sorry."

She shook her head, thinking about everything tumbling around in her head, everything she wanted and everything she'd waited so long for. Everything Cole had waited for, too.

"It's not the phone call. You didn't do anything wrong. You did everything right. I love you, Cole.

More than I have ever loved another man. I will never love anyone as much as I love you." She took his hand in hers. "Can we get married? Is that something you would consider?"

The corners of his mouth drew down. It was a full-on, no-doubt-about-it frown. "Dani, don't ask me that."

"What? Why not?"

He drew his legs up and swung them off the bed. "Because you're ruining my plan."

"Your plan? Why do you get to make a plan and I don't? I'm trying to make a plan for us, Cole. I thought that was what you wanted, too."

He paced over to the dresser, where his leather laptop bag was sitting. He must've been doing work at some point this evening. That was Cole. Ever the workaholic. He reached into the bag and turned around with a small gray box in his hand. "This is why you're ruining my plan." He handed her it to her and gathered his hands behind his back. "Go ahead. Open it," he said with a nod.

Certainly Dani wasn't lucky enough to have this many stars align all at once. Her heart was threatening to pound its way out of her chest as she tilted the top back. Inside, sat a beautiful, sparkly diamond solitaire.

"I don't want to sound like I'm copying you, but I love you, Dani. I don't want to waste another day not having you as my wife. We belong together. As a family."

Dani looked down at the ring. "You've been busy all day. When did you have time to buy this?"

"Is that your way of saying yes?" The expectation in Cole's eyes was enough to make her melt. He took the box from her hand and plucked the ring out of its home. "It's not hard. You just say.something like, 'Yes, Cole Sullivan, I *will* marry you. I *will* be your wife.'" He batted his lashes at her mockingly.

Dani laughed. How she loved their back-and-forth. "It is a stunning ring," she said, messing with him a little bit.

He slid the ring on to her finger. "It looks good on your hand. It fits perfectly." He then cast his mesmerizing eyes down at her with an expression she couldn't fully describe. "Here's where I make my full confession, Dani. I bought you this ring a week before my accident. Six years ago. I was all ready to ask you to marry me, and like a fool, I let our life together slip away. I'm not going to let that happen again. I can't offer you a lifetime, but I can offer you *my* lifetime. Whether I have fifty years or fifty minutes in me, I don't know. I only know that every second of it that we're not together is a second wasted."

The tears had turned to a steady stream. She'd once thought she could never get past the hurt of everything that had happened between them, but this step forward not only healed, it made them stronger. "I will marry you, Cole Sullivan. I want nothing more than to be your wife."

He pulled her close and gave her his trademark kiss—soft and sensuous and so potent she couldn't think straight. "That is music to my ears. I've never wanted to hear anything as much as I wanted to hear that."

She set her head on his shoulder and admired her ring when she flattened her hand against his chest. "I've never been happier to say something."

"So, I've been thinking since this morning. Just about everything else that we need to talk about." Cole traced his fingers up and down Dani's spine. "I want you and the boys to move out to the ranch. I know it's a lot to ask, but it's been in my family for generations and it would mean a lot to me."

How could she possibly refuse such a heartfelt request? She couldn't. She gazed up into his eyes. "Yes. Of course."

Cole rewarded her with a sensuous kiss that made her knees wobble. "I was thinking that with you, Elena and the boys living out at the ranch, there won't be nearly enough room for my parents when they come to visit. I was thinking we could have them stay here. Many miles away from the ranch."

"Good God, you're sexy when you're brilliant." Cole's parents had certainly mellowed, but that didn't mean she wanted them around all the time. Visits could be nice.

"We still need to talk about your job, Cole. I just can't deal with you doing dangerous stuff all the time. It'll kill me. I know you're not really a desk job kind of guy, but surely there's some compromise somewhere. Somehow."

He was grinning like a fool, which usually meant

he had something up his sleeve. "I'm way ahead of you. I've already decided I'm just going to do the investigative part of my job as soon as this case is done. It's not good for me, anyway. The doctor wants me avoiding stress."

"You know what's good for alleviating stress?" Dani drew her finger down Cole's chest, then leaned in for another kiss.

"I feel calmer already. Just imagine how great I'll feel after you get out of that chef's coat and into something more naked."

The door behind Cole cracked open. Dani and Cole both jumped. "Mommy?" Cameron croaked. "I woke up and I can't get back to sleep."

"It's okay, buddy. Maybe we can read one more story and then head back to bed," Cole said. "But we'd better read it in here so we don't wake up your brother. Do you think you can tiptoe into your room and get a book?"

Cameron nodded eagerly and rushed out into the hall.

"Hey. I'm sorry," Dani said. "This shouldn't ruin our plans tonight. He should go back to sleep pretty easily."

"They're our children, Dani. If you think I'm feeling put out, I'm not. I actually feel great." He smiled and pulled her into his warm embrace. "I have two sweet boys and the sexiest, most incredible woman on the planet." He punctuated his sweet statement with another soft kiss. "I can't wait to be married to you."

"I can't wait, either. I love you so much." She pulled him even closer, their gazes connected, and she reached down to grab his magnificent butt, giving it a nongentle squeeze. "And as soon as Cameron goes back to bed, I vote we start practicing for the honeymoon."

* * * * *

Don't miss a single installment of the.
TEXAS CATTLEMAN'S CLUB:
THE IMPOSTOR
*Will the scandal of the century lead to love for
these rich ranchers?*

*THE RANCHER'S BABY by New York Times
bestselling author Maisey Yates.*

RICH RANCHER'S REDEMPTION by
USA TODAY *bestselling author Maureen Child.*

*A CONVENIENT TEXAS WEDDING
by Sheri WhiteFeather.*

EXPECTING A SCANDAL by Joanne Rock.

REUNITED...WITH BABY by
USA TODAY *bestselling author Sara Orwig.*

THE NANNY PROPOSAL by Joss Wood.

*SECRET TWINS FOR THE TEXAN
by Karen Booth.*

LONE STAR SECRETS by Cat Schield.

***

*If you're on Twitter, tell us what you think
of Harlequin Desire! #harlequindesire*

From New York Times *bestselling author Maisey Yates comes the sizzling second book in her new* GOLD VALLEY *Western romance series. Shy tomboy Kaylee Capshaw never thought she'd have a chance of winning the heart of her longtime friend Bennett Dodge, even if he is the cowboy of her dreams.*

But when she learns he's suddenly single, can she finally prove to him that the woman he's been waiting for has been right here all along?

Read on for a sneak peek at
UNTAMED COWBOY,
the latest in New York Times
bestselling author Maisey Yates's
GOLD VALLEY *series!*

CHAPTER ONE

KAYLEE CAPSHAW NEEDED a new life. Which was why she was steadfastly avoiding the sound of her phone vibrating in her purse while the man across from her at the beautifully appointed dinner table continued to talk, oblivious to the internal war raging inside of her.

Do not look at your phone.

The stern internal admonishment didn't help. Everything in her was still seized up with adrenaline and anxiety over the fact that she had texts she wasn't looking at.

Not because of her job. Any and all veterinary emergencies were being covered by her new assistant at the clinic, Laura, so that she could have this date with Michael, the perfectly nice man she was now ignoring while she warred within herself to *not look down at her phone*.

No. It wasn't work texts she was itching to look at.

But what if it was Bennett?

Laura knew that she wasn't supposed to interrupt Kaylee tonight, because Kaylee was on a date, but she had conveniently not told Bennett. Because she didn't want to talk to Bennett about her dating anyone.

Mostly because she didn't want to hear if Bennett was dating anyone. If the woman lasted, Kaylee would inevitably know all about her. So there was no reason—in her mind—to rush into all of that.

She wasn't going to look at her phone.

"Going over the statistical data for the last quarter was really very interesting. It's fascinating how the holidays inform consumers."

Kaylee blinked. "What?"

"Sorry. I'm probably boring you. The corporate side of retail at Christmas is probably only interesting to people who work in the industry."

"Not at all," she said. Except, she wasn't interested. But she was trying to be. "How exactly did you get involved in this job living here?"

"Well, I can do most of it online. Sometimes I travel to Portland, which is where the corporate office is." Michael worked for a world-famous brand of sports gear, and he did something with the sales. Or data.

Her immediate attraction to him had been his dachshund, Clarence, whom she had seen for a tooth abscess a couple of weeks earlier. Then on a follow-up visit he had asked if Kaylee would like to go out, and she had honestly not been able to think of one good reason she shouldn't. Except for Bennett

Dodge. Her best friend since junior high and the obsessive focus of her hormones since she'd discovered what men and women did together in the dark.

Which meant she absolutely needed to go out with Michael.

Bennett couldn't be the excuse. Not anymore.

She had fallen into a terrible rut over the last couple of years while she and Bennett had gotten their clinic up and running. Work and her social life revolved around him. Social gatherings were all linked to him and to his family.

She'd lived in Gold Valley since junior high, and the friendships she'd made here had mostly faded since then. She'd made friends when she'd gone to school for veterinary medicine, but she and Bennett had gone together, and those friends were mostly mutual friends.

If they ever came to town for a visit, it included Bennett. If she took a trip to visit them, it often included Bennett.

The man was up in absolutely everything, and the effects of it had been magnified recently as her world had narrowed thanks to their mutually demanding work schedule.

That amount of intense, focused time with him never failed to put her in a somewhat pathetic emotional space.

Hence the very necessary date.

Then her phone started vibrating because it was ringing, and she couldn't ignore that. "I'm sorry," she said. "Excuse me."

It was Bennett. Her heart slammed into her throat. She should not answer it. She really shouldn't. She thought that even while she was pressing the green accept button.

"What's up?" she asked.

"Calving drama. I have a breech one. I need some help."

Bennett sounded clipped and stressed. And he didn't stress easily. He delivered countless calves over the course of the season, but a breech birth was never good. If the rancher didn't call him in time, there was rarely anything that could be done.

And if Bennett needed some assistance, then the situation was probably pretty extreme.

"Where are you?" she asked, darting a quick look over to Michael and feeling like a terrible human for being marginally relieved by this interruption.

"Out of town at Dave Miller's place. Follow the driveway out back behind the house."

"See you soon." She hung up the phone and looked down at her half-finished dinner. "I am so sorry," she said, forcing herself to look at Michael's face. "There's a veterinary emergency. I have to go."

She stood up, collecting her purse and her jacket. "I really am sorry. I tried to cover everything. But my partner… It's a barnyard thing. He needs help."

Michael looked… Well, he looked understanding. And Kaylee almost wished that he wouldn't. That he would be mad so that she would have an excuse to storm off and never have dinner with him again. That he would be unreasonable in some fashion so that she could call the date experiment a loss and go back to making no attempts at a romantic life whatsoever.

But he didn't. "Of course," he said. "You can't let something happen to an animal just because you're on a dinner date."

"I really can't," she said. "I'm sorry."

She reached into her purse and pulled out a twenty-dollar bill. She put it on the table and offered an apologetic smile before turning and leaving. Before he didn't accept her contribution to the dinner.

She was not going to make him pay for the entire meal on top of everything.

"Have a good evening," the hostess said as Kaylee walked toward the front door of the restaurant. "Please dine with us again soon."

Kaylee muttered something and headed outside, stumbling a little bit when her kitten heel caught in a crack in the sidewalk. That was the highest heel she ever wore, since she was nearly six feet tall in flats, and towering over one's date was not the best first impression.

But she was used to cowgirl boots and not these spindly, fiddly things that hung up on every imperfection. They were impractical. How any woman walked around in stilettos was beyond her.

The breeze kicked up, reminding her that March could not be counted on for warm spring weather as the wind stung her bare legs. The cost of wearing a dress. Which also had her feeling pretty stupid right about now.

She always felt weird in dresses, owing that to

her stick figure and excessive height. She'd had to be tough from an early age. With parents who ultimately ended up ignoring her existence, she'd had to be self-sufficient.

It had suited her to be a tomboy because spending time outdoors, running around barefoot and climbing trees, far away from the fight scenes her parents continually staged in their house, was better than sitting at home.

Better to pretend she didn't like lace and frills, since her bedroom consisted of a twin mattress on the floor and a threadbare afghan.

She'd had a friend when she was little, way before they'd moved to Gold Valley, who'd had the prettiest princess room on earth. Lace bedding, a canopy. Pink walls with flower stencils. She'd been so envious of it. She'd felt nearly sick with it.

But she'd just said she hated girlie things. And never invited that friend over ever.

And hey, she'd been built for it. Broad shoulders and stuff.

Sadly, she *wasn't* built for pretty dresses.

But she needed strength more, anyway.

She was thankful she had driven her own truck, which was parked not far down the street against the curb. First-date rule for her. Drive your own vehicle. In case you had to make a hasty getaway.

And apparently she had needed to make a hasty getaway, just not because Michael was a weirdo or anything.

No, he had been distressingly nice.

She mused on that as she got into the driver's seat and started the engine. She pulled away from the curb and headed out of town. Yes, he had been perfectly nice. Really, there had been nothing wrong with him. And she was a professional at finding things wrong with the men she went on dates with. A professional at finding excuses for why a second date couldn't possibly happen.

She was ashamed to realize now that she was hoping he would consider this an excuse not to make a second date with her.

That she had taken a phone call in the middle of dinner and then had run off.

A lot of people had trouble dating. But often it was for deep reasons they had trouble identifying.

Kaylee knew exactly why she had trouble dating.

It was because she was in love with her best friend, Bennett Dodge. And he was *not* in love with her.

She gritted her teeth.

She wasn't in love with Bennett. No. She wouldn't allow that. She had lustful feelings for Bennett, and she cared deeply about him. But she wasn't in love with him. She refused to let it be that. Not anymore.

That thought carried her over the gravel drive that led to the ranch, back behind the house, just as Bennett had instructed. The doors to the barn were flung open, the lights on inside, and she recognized Bennett's truck parked right outside.

She killed the engine and got out, then moved into the barn as quickly as possible.

"What's going on?" she asked.

Dave Miller was there, his arms crossed over his chest, standing back against the wall. Bennett had his hand on the cow's back. He turned to look at her, the overhead light in the barn seeming to shine a halo around his cowboy hat. That chiseled face that she knew so well but never failed to make her stomach go tight. He stroked the cow, his large, capable hands drawing her attention, as well as the muscles in his forearm. He was wearing a tight T-shirt that showed off the play of those muscles to perfection. His large biceps and the scars on his skin from various on-the-job injuries. He had a stethoscope draped over his shoulders, and something about that combination—rough-and-ready cowboy meshed with concerned veterinarian—was her very particular catnip.

"I need to get the calf out as quickly as possible, and I need to do it at the right moment. Too quickly and we're likely to crush the baby's ribs." She had a feeling he said that part for the benefit of the nervous-looking rancher standing off to the side.

Dave Miller was relatively new to town, having moved up from California a couple of years ago with fantasies of rural living. A small ranch for him and his wife's retirement had grown to a medium-sized one over the past year or so. And while the older man had a reputation for taking great care of his animals, he wasn't experienced at this.

"Where do you want me?" she asked, moving over to where Bennett was standing.

"I'm going to need you to suction the hell out of

this thing as soon as I get her out." He appraised her. "Where were you?"

"It doesn't matter."

"You're wearing a dress."

She shrugged. "I wasn't at home."

He frowned. "Were you out?"

This was not the time for Bennett to go overly concerned big brother on her. It wasn't charming on a normal day, but it was even less charming when she'd just abandoned her date to help deliver a calf. "If I wasn't at home, I was out. Better put your hand up the cow, Bennett," she said, feeling testy.

Bennett did just that, checking to see that the cow was dilated enough for him to extract the calf. Delivering a breech animal like this was tricky business. They were going to have to pull the baby out, likely with the aid of a chain or a winch, but not *too* soon, which would injure the mother. And not too quickly, which would injure them both.

But if they went too slow, the baby cow would end up completely cut off from its oxygen supply. If that happened, it was likely to never recover.

"Ready," he said. "I need chains."

She looked around and saw the chains lying on the ground, then she picked them up and handed them over. He grunted and pulled, producing the first hint of the calf's hooves. Then he lashed the chain around them. He began to pull again, his muscles straining against the fabric of his black T-shirt, flexing as he tugged hard.

She had been a vet long enough that she was inured to things like this, from a gross-out-factor perspective. But still, checking out a guy in the midst of all of this was probably a little imbalanced. Of course, that was the nature of how things were with her and Bennett.

They'd met when she'd moved to Gold Valley at thirteen—all long limbs, anger and adolescent awkwardness. And somehow, they'd fit. He'd lost his mother when he was young, and his family was limping along. Her own home life was hard, and she'd been desperate for escape from her parents' neglect and drunken rages at each other.

She never had him over. She didn't want to be at her house. She never wanted him, or any other friend, to see the way her family lived.

To see her sad mattress on the floor and her peeling nightstand.

Instead, they'd spent time at the Dodge ranch. His family had become hers, in many ways. They weren't perfect, but there was more love in their broken pieces than Kaylee's home had ever had.

He'd taught her to ride horses, let her play with the barn cats and the dogs that lived on the ranch. Together, the two of them had saved a baby squirrel that had been thrown out of his nest, nursing him back to health slowly in a little shoebox.

She'd blossomed because of him. Had discovered her love of animals. And had discovered she had the power to fix some of the broken things in the world.

The two of them had decided to become veterinarians together after they'd successfully saved the squirrel. And Bennett had never wavered.

He was a constant. A sure and steady port in the storm of life.

And when her feelings for him had started to shift and turn into more, she'd done her best to push them down because he was her whole world, and she didn't want to risk that by introducing anything as volatile as romance.

She'd seen how that went. Her parents' marriage was a reminder of just how badly all that could sour. It wasn't enough to make her swear off men, but it was enough to make her want to keep her relationship with Bennett as it was.

But that didn't stop the attraction.

If it were as simple as deciding not to want him, she would have done it a long time ago. And if it were as simple as being with another man, that would have worked back in high school when she had committed to finding herself a prom date and losing her virginity so she could get over Bennett Dodge already.

It had not worked. And the sex had been disappointing.

So here she was, fixating on his muscles while he helped an animal give birth.

Maybe there wasn't a direct line between those two things, but sometimes it felt like it. If all other men could just…not be so disappointing in comparison to Bennett Dodge, things would be much easier.

She looked away from him, making herself useful, gathering syringes and anything she would need to clear the calf of mucus that might be blocking its airway. Bennett hadn't said anything, likely for Dave's benefit, but she had a feeling he was worried about the health of the heifer. That was why he needed her to see to the calf as quickly as possible, because he was afraid he would be giving treatment to its mother.

She spread a blanket out that was balled up and stuffed in the corner—unnecessary, but it was something to do. Bennett strained and gave one final pull and brought the calf down as gently as possible onto the barn floor.

"There he is," Bennett said, breathing heavily. "There he is."

His voice was filled with that rush of adrenaline that always came when they worked jobs like this.

She and Bennett ran the practice together, but she typically held down the fort at the clinic and treated smaller domestic animals like birds, dogs, cats and the occasional ferret.

Bennett worked with large animals, cows, horses, goats and sometimes llamas. They had a mobile unit for things like this.

But when push came to shove, they helped each other out.

And when push came to pulling a calf out of its mother, they definitely helped each other.

Bennett took care of the cord and then turned his focus back to the mother.

Kaylee moved to the calf, who was glassy-eyed and not looking very good. But she knew from her limited experience with this kind of delivery that just because they came out like this didn't mean they wouldn't pull through.

She checked his airway, brushing away any remaining mucus that was in the way. She put her hand back over his midsection and tried to get a feel on his heartbeat. "Bennett," she said, "stethoscope?"

"Here," he said, taking it from around his neck and tossing it her direction. She caught it and slipped the ear tips in, then pressed the diaphragm against the calf, trying to get a sense of what was happening in there.

His heartbeat sounded strong, which gave her hope.

His breathing was still weak. She looked around at the various tools, trying to see something she might be able to use. "Dave," she said to the man standing back against the wall. "I need a straw."

"A straw?"

"Yes. I've never tried this before, but I hear it works."

She had read that sticking a straw up a calf's nose irritated the system enough that it jolted them into breathing. And she hoped that was the case.

Dave returned quickly with the item that she had requested, and Kaylee moved the straw into position. Not gently, since that would defeat the purpose.

You had to love animals to be in her line of work. And unfortunately, loving them sometimes meant hurting them.

The calf startled, then heaved, his chest rising and falling deeply before he started to breathe quickly.

Kaylee pulled the straw out and lifted her hands. "Thank God."

Bennett turned around, shifting his focus to the calf and away from the mother. "Breathing?"

"Breathing."

He nodded, wiping his forearm over his forehead. "Good." His chest pitched upward sharply. "I think Mom is going to be okay, too."

UNTAMED COWBOY
by New York Times *bestselling author*
Maisey Yates,
available July 2018 wherever
HQN Books and ebooks are sold.
www.Harlequin.com

Get 4 **FREE REWARDS!**

We'll send you 2 FREE Books
<u>plus</u> 2 FREE Mystery Gifts.

Harlequin® Desire books feature heroes who have it all: wealth, status, incredible good looks... everything but the right woman.

FREE Value Over **$20**

Her mouth watered, not for the food, but for him.

Not why you came here, Miriam reminded herself sternly.

Yet here she stood. Chase had figured out—before she'd
admitted it to herself—that she'd come here not only to give
him a piece of her mind but also to give herself the comfort of
knowing he'd had a home-cooked meal on Thanksgiving.

She balled her fist as a flutter of desire took flight between her
thighs. She wanted to touch him. Maybe just once.

He pushed her wineglass closer to her. An offer.

An offer she wouldn't accept.

Couldn't accept.

She wasn't unlike Little Red Riding Hood, having run to the
wrong house for shelter. Only in this case, the Big Bad Wolf
wasn't dining on Red's beloved grandmother but Miriam's
family's home cooking.

An insistent niggling warned her that she could be next—and
hadn't this particular "wolf" already consumed her heart?

"So, I'm going to go."

When she grabbed her coat and stood, a warm hand grasped
her much cooler one. Chase's fingers stroked hers before lightly

squeezing, his eyes studying her for a long moment, his fork hovering over his unfinished dinner.

Finally, he said, "I'll see you out."

"That's not necessary."

He did as he pleased and stood, his hand on her lower back as he walked with her. Outside, the wind pushed against the front door, causing the wood to creak. She and Chase exchanged glances. Had she waited too long?

"For the record, I don't want you to leave."

What she'd have given to hear those words on that airfield ten years ago.

"I'll be all right."

"You can't know that." He frowned out of either concern or anger, she couldn't tell which.

"Stay." Chase's gray-green eyes were warm and inviting, his voice a time capsule back to not-so-innocent days. The request was siren-call sweet, but she'd not risk herself for it.

"No." She yanked open the front door, shocked when the howling wind shoved her back a few inches. Snow billowed in, swirling around her feet, and her now wet, cold fingers slipped from the knob.

Chase caught her, an arm looped around her back, and shoved the door closed with the flat of one palm. She hung there, suspended by the corded forearm at her back, clutching his shirt in one fist, and nearly drowned in his lake-colored eyes.

"I can stay for a while longer," she squeaked, the decision having been made for her.

His handsome face split into a brilliant smile.

Don't miss A Snowbound Scandal *by Jessica Lemmon,
part of her* **Dallas Billionaires Club** *series!*

*Available August 2018 wherever
Harlequin® Desire books and ebooks are sold.*

www.Harlequin.com

Want to give in to temptation with
steamy tales of irresistible desire?

Check out **Harlequin® Presents®**,
Harlequin® Desire and
Harlequin® Kimani™ Romance books!

New books available every month!

CONNECT WITH US AT:

Harlequin.com/Community

 Facebook.com/HarlequinBooks

 Twitter.com/HarlequinBooks

 Instagram.com/HarlequinBooks

 Pinterest.com/HarlequinBooks

ReaderService.com

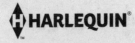 **HARLEQUIN®**

**ROMANCE WHEN
YOU NEED IT**

PGENRE2017

LOVE
Harlequin
romance?

Join our Harlequin community to share your thoughts and connect with other romance readers!

Be the first to find out about promotions, news, and exclusive content!

Sign up for the Harlequin e-newsletter and download a free book from any series at

www.TryHarlequin.com

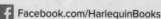

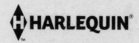